IS That an ANGRY PenGuin IN Your Gym BaG?

TODD STRASSER

P9-BYX-321

SCHOLASTIC INC.

New York Toronto London Auckland
Sydney Mexico City New Delhi Hong Kong

ISBN-13: 978-0-439-77697-4
ISBN-10: 0-439-77697-X

15 14 13 12 11 10 9 8 7 6 5 4   9 10 11 12 13 14/0

Printed in the U.S.A.   40
This edition first printing, November 2009

This book is dedicated to Howard Head, a brilliant inventor who helped revolutionize two of my favorite sports — tennis and skiing — and thus gave joy to millions of people around the world.

Thank you, Mr. Head.

T.S.

IS THAT AN ANGRY PENGUIN IN YOUR GYM BAG?

AUTHOR'S NOTE

    Welcome, faithful reader, to the wonderful world of the Tardy Boys. There are now 592 books in this world-famous series, making it THE LONGEST SERIES IN HISTORY! This is the fourth book, so you only have 588 books to go. You will be able to read book number five just as soon as the author gets around to writing it. Don't worry about having time to read them all because, as you probably know, the Tardy Boys is not only the world's longest book series, but also the world's fastest series. Many readers have reported finishing Is That a Dead Dog in Your Locker? and Is That a

Sick Cat in Your Backpack? in under one hour. Most recently, Evan Diddinblink of One, Mississippi, reported finishing Is That a Glow-in-the-Dark Bunny in Your Pillowcase? in just under fifty-four minutes.

Way to go, Evan!

In other news, the Tardy Boys have joined the protest movement against astronomers who want to take away Pluto's status as a planet. The author agrees that it was very unfair of astronomers to let Pluto think it was a planet all these years and then suddenly say it's not. What did Pluto ever do to them? How would they like to be a frozen rock at the edge of the solar system?

Finally, the author is excited to announce that he will be auditioning for American Super Mega Idol Star Search when it comes to his hometown. The author is certain that he, and only he, will be America's next Super Mega Idol Star because his mother says he should be. True that.

WARNING

If you have read other Tardy Boys books, you know that the author guarantees that you will not find the words UNDERPANTS or UNDERWEAR anywhere in this story. The author regrets that the same cannot be said for the words, Thunderwear®™ and Thunderpants®™. These words are the registered trademarks (®™) of the United Thunderwear®™ Corporation and cannot be used without the express written permission of the owners of the United Thunderwear®™ Corporation or their employees.

Since those words appear in this book, that must mean that someone in these pages either owns or works for the United Thunderwear®™ Corporation. The author isn't sure who that person is, but whoever it is, he probably wears Thunderpants®™, which differ from underpants in many important ways. As you know, underpants are worn under pants. Thunderpants®™ serve a completely different purpose. They are used for sound absorption and dampening.

THE MYSTERY OF THE HAIRY PAIR OF UNRULY PEAR-EATING HARES

It was a winter morning. The warm sun was rising and little red buds were starting to appear on the bare branches of the trees. In the Tardy Boys' front yard, the first green shoots of crocus and daffodils were poking up through the ground around the broken bicycles, smashed skateboards, bent Razor scooters, partly burned sofas, and broken toilets. Robins were hopping through the bright green grass looking for worms.

Yes, it was a winter morning. But thanks to global warming, by seven A.M. it was already seventy-five degrees.

"It's a good thing we have an indoor ice rink at The School With No Name," said Wade Tardy as he lugged his heavy hockey bag into the kitchen. "Otherwise, we'd be skating on thin ice."

"Or swimming," said his nonidentical twin brother, Leyton.

On this balmy winter morning, both Wade and Leyton were wearing shorts and T-shirts. Wade was thin and scrawny with dark unruly hair, and a skull packed with brain cells. Leyton was handsome, muscular, and had beautiful, flowing blond locks. For most of his life he had believed that his skull was so empty that monkeys could swing from tree branch to tree branch inside of it. But then, in book number three of this fabulous and groundbreaking series, Daisy Peduncle proved that inside Leyton's skull were just as many brain cells as everyone else had.

The Tardy Boy's younger brother, TJ, came into the kitchen wearing jeans, a hoodie, and a heavy jacket.

"Why are you dressed like that?" Wade asked him.

"Because it's winter," answered TJ. "Why are you wearing shorts and T-shirts?"

"Because it's going to be eighty-five degrees this afternoon," said Wade.

"How can it be eighty-five degrees in the middle of winter?" asked TJ.

"That's what global warming is all about, little dude," said Leyton. "You better go change or you'll be really hot and uncomfortable at school today."

TJ left to change his clothes. Wade looked at his dark, unruly hair in the kitchen mirror. It poked out from his head like tree branches. He tried to comb it, but it quickly returned to its unruly condition. "I don't understand why my hair won't stay combed," he complained.

"Maybe it doesn't want to," said Leyton, who never had to comb his perfectly managable, flowing blond locks because they were always . . . well, perfect.

"How can hair not *want* to stay combed?" asked Wade. "Hair doesn't have a mind of its own."

"Sure it does," said Leyton. "You used to say I had hair-brained ideas. That proves that hair has brains."

"No, Leyton," said Wade. "It's not hair-brained. It's *hare*brained. A hare is a rabbit. So something that's harebrained has the brains of a rabbit."

Leyton looked at himself in the kitchen mirror. "My hair isn't a rabbit. My hair is hair."

Wade stared at his brother in disbelief. It was still hard for him to accept that Leyton's head was filled with brain cells. "The hair on your head is spelled H-A-I-R. A hare that's a rabbit is spelled H-A-R-E. They're two different words, and they mean two different things. Like pear and pair."

"But you could have a pair of pears," Leyton said. "And don't hares have hair? So you could have a hairy pair of unruly pear-eating hares."

Just then the doorbell rang.

"You better go see who that is," said Wade.

Leyton didn't have to. Now that he had brains, he knew who it was. "It's Daisy."

"Then let her in," said Wade.

"Why don't you let her in?" Leyton said. Another advantage of having brains was knowing that Wade could no longer boss him around.

In frustration, Wade crossed his arms and pressed his chin against his chest. "It's not fair."

"What's not fair?" asked Leyton.

"It's not fair that you're good-looking and blond and muscular *and* have brains," said Wade. "While I'm scrawny and not so good-looking and have unruly hair."

Just then Daisy Peduncle, the fairest girl in all the land, walked into the kitchen and said, "Not all hair is fair."

BOX JELLYFISH

"By fair, do you mean, just and honest?" asked Leyton. "Or do you mean attractive and pleasing in appearance?"

"I meant that not all hair is fair-haired," said Daisy.

Daisy was wearing a yellow sundress and purple granny glasses. Her long, blonde, fair hair was bare. She was carrying a clipboard with some papers she wanted to share.

"Then you mean fair-haired as in light-colored hair," said Wade. "Which means I have unruly, unfair hair. And that's really unfair."

"Life isn't always fair, Wade," said Daisy. "For the past two hundred years, humans have been pumping greenhouse gases into the air. But it is only our generation that will have to beware."

"What if we don't care?" Leyton asked.

"Then we'll be in for a scare," said Wade.

"Stop it!" said TJ, who entered the kitchen wearing shorts and a T-shirt.

"Stop what?" asked Daisy.

"You're talking in rhymes again," TJ said.

"Sorry," said Wade.

"Have you tried combing your hair?" Daisy asked him.

"Like a thousand times," replied Wade.

"Then you may have CUHS," said Daisy. "Chronic Unruly Hair Syndrome."

"Is that bad?" asked Leyton.

"Not as bad as global warming," said Daisy. She handed them the clipboard. "That's why you should sign my petition for increased production of ethanol."

"What's ethanol?" asked TJ.

"It's fuel made from corn," Daisy explained. "It puts fewer greenhouse gases in the atmosphere. And that could help slow global warming."

"Sounds cool," said TJ.

"Yes, it will help keep the world cooler than if we continue to use gasoline," said Daisy.

"I'm not sure that's what TJ meant," said Wade. "Is there a cure for CUHS?"

"Have you tried mousse?" asked Daisy.

"No, but I once had a bison burger," said Wade.

"Not moose," said Daisy. "Mousse. For your hair."

"I've tried everything," said Wade, "styling gel, hair spray, hair wax, pomade, headbands, hair clips, and hair wraps."

"I know a hair rap," said TJ, and chanted:

YO, BRO, YOU BETTER BEWARE,

MY HOMIES AND ME, WE GOT SOME HAIR.

AND IF THAT HAIR, IT AIN'T THERE,

THEN YOU BETTER BE WEARING

THUNDERWEAR®™.

Daisy put her hand on TJ's forehead to see if he was running a fever. But he felt normal.

"It's time to go to school," said Wade.

The Tardy Boys heaved up their heavy hockey bags. Daisy grabbed her petition, and they all left the house. Outside, the round, early morning yellow sun shined in the sky and birds chirped in the trees. Black-and-yellow butterflies fluttered by. Joggers passed wearing sweatbands and carrying water bottles.

Lugging their hockey bags, Wade and Leyton began to sweat.

"I like hockey, but I sure don't like carrying this heavy bag," Leyton said, wiping the sweat from his forehead.

"It wouldn't be so bad if it weren't for this heat," said Wade.

"If it's this warm in February, what will July be like?" asked TJ.

"With global warming, it's impossible to know," someone said. The Tardy Boys and Daisy turned to see their friend Al-Ian

Konspiracy coming toward them carrying a hockey bag. Al-Ian was a friendly boy and a brainiac who believed in aliens and UFOs. Al-Ian was wearing his black Velostat Thought-Screen Helmet, which was specially designed to stop aliens from reading his mind and controlling his thoughts. He was also wearing his Intergalactic Return Address Dog Tags in case he had to find his way home from a distant planet in a faraway galaxy, and his football shoulder pads covered with aluminum foil to deflect alien body heat sensor rays.

"Do you know what I just realized, Al-Ian?" Leyton asked.

"That the world's most poisonous creature is the box jellyfish of Australia?" Al-Ian guessed.

"No," said Leyton.

"That the box jellyfish has ninety-six eyes, but no brain?" Al-Ian guessed.

"Not that, either," said Leyton. "What I just realized is that since you are already wearing that helmet and those shoulder pads, all you'll have to do is put on a hockey jersey and you'll be ready to play hockey."

"And you might *not* be surprised to learn that football and hockey players are the professional athletes who are least likely to be abducted by alien sports scouts," said Al-Ian.

At the next corner, TJ said good-bye and headed toward the elementary school.

"Want to know what's surprising?" asked Wade as he and the others continued toward The School With No Name.

"That sea turtles are immune to the venom of box jellyfish and like to eat them for lunch?" guessed Al-Ian.

"No," said Wade. "What's surprising is that we've gotten this far in our morning walk without being attacked by our WORST ARCHENEMY EVER."

"Look out!" Leyton shouted.

THE KILLER JOKE

Barton Slugg, the Tardy Boys' WORST
ARCHENEMY EVER, stepped out onto the
sidewalk in front of them. But this was
not the OLD Barton, whose feet reeked
of stinky toe cheese. This was not even
the NEW Barton, whose feet no longer
reeked. This was THE NEW AND
IMPROVED Barton. He still had buckteeth and brown hair that fell into his

eyes. And he was still the biggest slimeball ever. But THE NEW AND IMPROVED Barton now knew that pretty was not spelled pritty.

The Tardy Boys dropped their hockey bags. They cowered on the sidewalk, awaiting Barton's latest attack. In the past, Barton had trapped them with slime ice, the superslippery ice caused by his horrible toe cheese. He had bombarded them with perfect round snowballs from his Super Slammer snowball gun.

But now that it was seventy-five degrees, there was no ice for slime ice and no snow for snowballs.

And that could only mean one thing — THE NEW AND IMPROVED Barton had to have a NEW AND IMPROVED weapon!

Trembling in fear, the Tardy Boys and Daisy wondered if it would be:

a. The Terrible Green Snot Slingshot?

b. The Horrible Long Distance Spit Sprayer?

c. The Awful Garlic-and-Onion Bad Breathalyzer?

d. Something Even Worse?

e. All of the above?

Finally, Wade couldn't take the stress a second more. "Tell us, Barton! What terrible, horrible thing are you going to do to us this time?"

THE NEW AND IMPROVED Barton narrowed his eyes. He bared his big buckteeth. "Why did the monkey fall out of the tree?"

The Tardy Boys and their friends glanced fearfully at one another. Was this some kind of secret code? Were there monkeys in the trees around them? Were they Attack Monkeys trained by Barton to attack his enemies?

THE NEW AND IMPROVED Barton repeated the question, "Why did the monkey fall out of the tree?"

Unable to stand the suspense any longer, Leyton said, "We don't know! Why?"

"Because he was dead," said Barton.

The Tardy Boys and their friends glanced around in fear. They were certain something terrible was going to happen. But nothing did. Finally, Wade said, "I don't get it."

"It's a joke," said Barton. "You're supposed to laugh."

"But it wasn't funny," said Daisy.

"Yes, it was," said Barton.

"No, it wasn't," said Al-Ian.

THE NEW AND IMPROVED Barton grit his teeth and snarled. "Why did the *second* monkey fall out of the tree?"

"How would we know?" said Daisy.

"Because he was stapled to the first monkey," said Barton.

The Tardy Boys groaned.

THE NEW AND IMPROVED Barton smiled sadistically. "Why did the *third* monkey fall out of the tree?"

This time no one answered.

"He thought it was a race to the bottom," said Barton.

"Those jokes are so bad, they hurt," said Leyton.

THE NEW AND IMPROVED Barton grinned an evil grin. "Why did the *fourth* monkey fall out of the tree?"

"Stop!" begged Wade.

"He was playing follow the leader," said Barton.

Al-Ian covered his ears. "I can't take it anymore!"

But THE NEW AND IMPROVED Barton wouldn't stop. "Why did the *fifth* monkey fall out of the tree?"

"Please don't tell us!" Daisy begged.

"He didn't know which way was up," said Barton.

"Ahhhhh!" The Tardy Boys and their friends fell to the ground, covering their ears with their hands and writhing in pain.

It was now clear what THE NEW AND IMPROVED Barton's NEW AND IMPROVED *weapon* was: the Killer Joke!

THE NEXT AMERICAN SUPER MEGA IDOL STAR

"Give up?" asked Barton.

"Yes!" gasped Wade.

"We surrender," moaned Daisy.

"You've finally done it," grimaced Al-Ian. "You've totally defeated us."

Barton smiled. "You really thought those jokes were *that* bad?"

"The worst," Leyton said as he staggered to his feet.

"We understand why you'd want to massacre us with your killer joke," Wade said. "But why try to harm Daisy? We thought you liked her."

A tiny tear formed in the corner of Barton's eye, but he quickly wiped it away and said nothing.

"Promise us you won't tell any more jokes like that?" said Daisy.

"I'll promise," Barton said. "On one condition."

"We invite you to all our parties?" Daisy guessed.

"No," said Barton.

"We let you have all our Halloween candy forever?" guessed Leyton.

"No," said Barton.

"We promise never to read your poetry again?" guessed Al-Ian.

"No," said Barton. "I want you to promise . . . that you won't audition for *American Super Mega Idol Star Search*."

"Huh?" The Tardy Boys and their friends frowned.

"What do you mean?" asked Wade.

"Didn't you read the newspaper this morning?" Barton asked. "That TV show, *American Super Mega Idol Star Search*, is coming to our town tonight to find the next American Super Mega Idol Star. And I don't want any of you trying out for it."

"Why not?" asked Daisy.

"Because I want to win," said Barton.

"What are you going to try out as?" Al-Ian asked.

"Guess," said Barton.

"A singer?" Wade guessed.

"Nope."

"A dancer?" asked Daisy.

"Nope."

"An inventor?" guessed Al-Ian.

"Nope."

"Then what?" asked Leyton.

Barton grinned. "A comedian."

"But you're the worst comedian ever," said Wade.

Barton smirked. "You haven't heard my good stuff."

"Yeah, but we've heard your *bad* stuff," said Al-Ian. "And it's so bad that even your good stuff will have to be awful."

Barton squinted angrily. "Why did the *sixth* monkey fall out of the tree?"

"Run!" Wade yelled.

A CERTIFIABLE WHACK JOB

The Tardy Boys grabbed their hockey bags, then with their friends, ran the rest of the way to The School With No Name. When they got there, they noticed that some things were the same, but other things were different.

The same: Ulna Mandible was screaming at Principal Stratemeyer and Assistant Principal Snout. Her daughter,

Fibby, stood behind her with her arms crossed and a smile on her face.

Different: Instead of his blue suit, Principal Stratemeyer was wearing a short-sleeve green-and-yellow Hawaiian shirt and khaki shorts because it was going to be eighty-five degrees that day and, since he was the top banana at The School With No Name, he could wear whatever he wanted.

The same: Assistant Principal Snout was wearing yellow earplugs, a white breathing mask, and blue latex gloves because he was a certifiable whack job.

Different: The school's ice rink was surrounded by a SWAT team of police officers wearing dark blue helmets and body armor, and carrying black assault weapons.

"What do you mean, my daughter can't take her figure skating lesson this morning?" Ulna shrieked at the principals. "How is she going to win the *American Super Mega Idol Star Search* tonight if she can't practice?"

"I'm sorry, Mrs. Mandible," said Assistant Principal Snout, "but the police have sealed off the ice skating rink because it has been taken over by small, flightless, birdlike black-and-white aliens."

"Did you hear that!?" gasped Al-Ian, who became excited whenever aliens were mentioned.

"I don't believe you," Ulna Mandible screamed at the assistant principal. "I think you've closed the skating rink because *you* want to win the *American Super Mega Idol Star Search* yourself."

"That can't be true, Mrs. Mandible," Principal Stratemeyer said in a calm voice. "In order to enter the *American Super Mega Idol Star Search*, Assistant Principal Snout would have to take off his gloves, earplugs, and breathing mask in public. And he hasn't done that in more than seven years."

"Besides," said Assistant Principal Snout, "the only talent I have is for punishing students who are late to school."

"And we all know how much talent that takes," added Principal Stratemeyer.

"I'm going to talk to my lawyer," shouted Ulna. "And believe me, if I can sue, I will!"

Ulna Mandible got into her big red Hummer and roared away. Principal

Stratemeyer and Fibby went into school. Assistant Principal Snout turned to the Tardy Boys and their friends and said, "Late again. What's your excuse this time?"

"We were attacked by Barton," said Al-Ian.

"What did he do?" asked the assistant principal.

"He tried to murder us with killer jokes," said Leyton.

Assistant Principal Snout's forehead wrinkled and his eyebrows dipped. He might have frowned, but it was impossible to tell because his mouth was hidden by the breathing mask. "That is the lamest excuse you've ever made up."

"But it's true!" Wade insisted.

"Oh, yeah?" said Assistant Principal Snout. "What was the joke?"

Daisy told him about the monkey falling out of the tree.

Assistant Principal Snout laughed. "That's funny!"

"No, it's not," said Al-Ian. "It's stupid."

"Oh, yeah?" said the assistant principal. "I'd like to see *you* come up with something funnier."

"Okay," said Al-Ian. "What do aliens wear to fancy weddings?"

No one knew.

"Space suits!" Al-Ian cried, then doubled over in laughter.

"That's not funny," said Assistant Principal Snout.

"Are you serious?" Al-Ian gasped. "It's hysterical!"

Assistant Principal Snout turned to the

Tardy Boys and Daisy. "Did you think it was funny?"

"Not really," said Wade.

Now Barton came down the sidewalk, toward The School With No Name.

"Why are you late?" Assistant Principal Snout asked him.

Barton pointed his finger at the Tardy Boys and their friends. "They stopped me."

"That's a lie!" said Leyton.

"Silence, Leyton," ordered Assistant Principal Snout. "How did they stop you, Barton?"

"They blocked my path and said I couldn't pass until I told a funny joke," Barton said.

"That's totally bogus!" gasped Wade.

"Silence, Wade," ordered Assistant Principal Snout. "What joke did you tell them, Barton?"

"Do you promise that you'll let me go into school even if you don't think it's funny?" Barton asked.

"Yes, I promise," said Assistant Principal Snout.

"Know why the boy threw the clock out the window?" asked Barton. "He wanted to see time fly."

"Everyone knows that joke," said Assistant Principal Snout. "It's not funny."

"But you promised I could go into school," said Barton.

"That's true," said Assistant Principal Snout. "And I always keep my promises. You may go into school." Then the assistant principal looked at the Tardy Boys and their friends. "I'll see you four in my office."

ALIEN HOCKEY PUCKS

The Tardy Boys and their friends went into The School With No Name.

"I can't believe Snout let Barton go even though he was later than we were!" Leyton complained.

"I can't believe the ice rink's been taken over by small, flightless, birdlike black-and-white aliens," said Al-Ian.

"I'm not so sure about that," said Daisy.

"Why not?" asked Wade.

"Did any of you see a spaceship?" Daisy asked.

"Snout said they were flightless," said Al-Ian.

The Tardy Boys and Daisy gave one another puzzled looks.

"That makes no sense, Al-Ian," said Daisy. "If they're really aliens then they *had* to fly here from another planet."

"Not true," said Al-Ian. "Maybe they *swam* through space."

"If you don't think they're aliens, then what do you think they are?" Wade asked Daisy.

"I'm not sure," said Daisy. "But what's small and black and loves ice?"

"A hockey puck!" Leyton realized.

"Alien hockey pucks from outer space!"

Al-Ian gasped. "The puck aliens from the Planet Disk in the Hard Rubber Galaxy!"

Daisy rolled her eyes. "They're not alien hockey pucks."

"How do *you* know?" Al-Ian asked.

"Well, for one thing, hockey pucks sometimes fly," Daisy said.

By now, they'd reached Assistant Principal Snout's office. Before they could go in, they had to leave their shoes on the mat outside the door and wash their hands in the sink.

While Wade washed his hands, he looked in the mirror above the sink. His hair was sticking out in practically every direction. *It's not fair that I have unruly hair,* he thought.

When they'd all removed their shoes and washed their hands, they entered the office. Immediately, the Tardy Boys and their friends noticed that some things were different, but others were the same.

The same: In the corner, a large, hypoallergenic air purifier hummed. On the shelf behind Assistant Principal Snout's desk were three large boxes. One contained white breathing masks. Another contained light blue latex gloves. The third contained bright yellow foam earplugs. Four chairs lined the wall as far from the assistant principal's desk as possible.

Different: The red line on the floor between the chairs and the desk was gone. Also missing was the sign that said:

STUDENTS DO NOT CROSS THIS LINE

Instead a thick clear pane of bullet- and soundproof glass now stretched from the floor to the ceiling. And on the wall beside Assistant Principal Snout's desk was a huge HDTV showing the twenty-four hour news station.

"What's this about?" Leyton asked, tapping his finger against the thick glass.

"Probably just another way for Snout to keep students from getting too close," said Wade.

On the other side of the office, a bookcase swung open. Assistant Principal Snout stepped through it.

"A secret doorway!" Al-Ian gasped.

The Tardy Boys and their friends watched as Assistant Principal Snout sat down at his desk and removed his bright yellow earplugs. Now that he was safe in his office, he did not have to fear THE SHRIEK OF ULNA MANDIBLE. He also took off his breathing mask. Now that he was in the same room with the hypoallergenic air purifier, he did not have to worry about breathing the same air students breathed. He also took off his blue latex gloves. Now that he was on the other side of the bulletproof glass, he did not have to worry about being touched by germ-ridden students.

Assistant Principal Snout picked up a telephone on his desk and dialed a number. A moment later, the Tardy Boys and their friends heard ringing on the wall behind them. They turned and discovered small telephone receivers. Assistant Principal Snout gestured for them to answer. The Tardy Boys and their friends picked up the phones.

"What are you doing in my office?" Assistant Principal Snout asked over the phone.

"You told us to come here," answered Daisy.

"Why?" asked Assistant Principal Snout.

"Because you said we were late," answered Wade.

"So? You're always late," said Assistant Principal Snout.

"We would have been on time today if Barton hadn't attacked us with his killer joke," said Leyton.

Assistant Principal Snout rubbed his chin and gazed at the HDTV. On the screen was a commercial for *American Super Mega Idol Star Search*. "Are any of you planning to audition?"

The Tardy Boys and their friends shook their heads.

"Why not?" asked Assistant Principal Snout. "Don't you want to be rich and famous and recognized everywhere you go?"

"I don't have to be a Super Mega Idol Star," said Al-Ian. "I'm happy just being me."

"There's something wrong when everybody thinks they have to be famous," said Daisy.

"If it ever got to a point where everyone was a star," said Wade, "then no one would be a star."

"Did you say rich *and* famous?" asked Leyton.

THE MYTH OF GLOBAL WARMING

Assistant Principal Snout nodded. Leyton turned to his friends. "Sounds pretty good to me."

"Then maybe you should audition," said Assistant Principal Snout.

Leyton knew that he'd have to have a talent to become a Super Mega Idol Star. He tried to think of what talents he had. He could eat Nurticat Deluxe with mustard and soy sauce. Now that his head was filled with brain cells, he sometimes had a good idea. Recently, he'd dug his own basement.

"I'm pretty good at digging," Leyton said.

Assistant Principal Snout shook his head. "Forget it. Stanley Yelnats has that category wrapped up."

Just then the secret doorway opened and Olga Shotput, the school's silver-medal–winning janitor, marched in and saluted Assistant Principal Snout. Olga was a large woman with short hair and muscular arms who had come to the United States many years ago to compete in the Spring Olympics. Only, there were no Spring Olympics.

"Assistant Principal Snout, sir," said Olga. "I believe I have finally earned a gold medal in custodianship!"

Assistant Principal Snout sighed. He had heard this request many times before. "Olga, you are a wonderful janitor. If there were such a thing as a gold medal in custodianship, I would give it to you. But there's no such thing."

Olga's shoulders sagged and she gazed down sadly at the silver medal that hung from her neck on a red, white, and blue ribbon. Only it wasn't really a medal, it was the top from a can of tuna fish. Her eyes began to water.

"Please don't cry, Olga," said Assistant Principal Snout. "Think of how few people in the world have won even a silver medal."

"But if I only have a silver medal in custodianship, how can I try out for *American Super Mega Idol Star Search?*" Olga sniffed. "Only a gold-medal janitor would have enough talent to win." She burst into tears.

Assistant Principal Snout got up from his desk and went to a closet. "Olga, I'm not sure whether I can help you become America's next Super Mega Idol Star, but I do want you to have this." He pulled out the biggest broom the Tardy Boys had ever seen.

"This is supposed to make me happy?" Olga sobbed, wiping the tears from her eyes. "A bigger broom?"

"Not just bigger, Olga," said Assistant Principal Snout. "*The biggest!* This is the special thirty-six-inch Thunderwear®™ Power Push Sweet Sweep Fine Bristle Push Broom."

"Whoop-de-do," Olga muttered with a sniff.

Assistant Principal Snout's eyes narrowed and it looked like he was going to get angry. But first, he got back on his phone with the Tardy Boys and their friends. "Go to class," he barked, and hung up.

The Tardy Boys and their friends left. When they got out to the hallway, Wade said, "That was strange."

"At least, we didn't get detention," said Al-Ian.

"I have to see what's in the skating rink," said Daisy.

"There's no way you can get past the SWAT teams," Al-Ian warned.

Just then, the office door opened and Olga Shotput trudged out, her head hanging and eyes red as she pushed her new thirty-six-inch Thunderwear®™

Power Push Sweet Sweep Fine Bristle Push Broom down the hall, dabbing her eyes with a tissue.

"I think I just got an idea," said Daisy. "Meet me at the rear entrance to the skating rink after next period. And bring some loud instruments."

"But we don't play any instruments," Leyton said.

"Doesn't matter," she said, and started away.

"Daisy, where are you going?" Al-Ian asked.

"Metal shop," she said.

The Tardy Boys and Al-Ian stuffed their hockey bags into their lockers, then they went to their first class of the day, which was Social Studies with Ms. Fitt. When they got to Ms. Fitt's room, they noticed a large, flat-screen HDTV on the wall. Ms.

Fitt was sitting at her desk, answering e-mails on her computer. She had red hair that hung down past her shoulders in ringlets. She liked to wear big earrings and colorful clothes. Today she was wearing a bright orange turtleneck sweater, a brown felt skirt, and green-and-white cowboy boots.

Wade raised his hand. "Where did all these televisions come from?"

"They were donated to our school by the National Association of Television Manufacturers," Ms. Fitt said.

"Why?" asked Al-Ian.

"Because recent studies have shown that watching television and movies in class is a helpful teaching tool," Ms. Fitt explained. "It creates a less stressful teaching environment, which helps teachers relax and gives them more time to do important things like answer e-mails and catch up on their sleep. You can learn a lot from watching TV."

"It's true," said one kid. "Until I saw *Jurassic Park*, I thought dinosaurs were extinct."

"But if we can learn everything we need to know from TV, why have school?" asked Leyton.

"We show fewer commercials," said Ms. Fitt. "Besides, if there was no school, what would teachers do?"

"Are we going to watch TV today?" asked Al-Ian.

"Yes," said their teacher. "I've just received a special DVD from the National Association of Coal and Oil Distributors."

"What's it called?" asked Wade.

"*The Myth of Global Warming,*" said Ms. Fitt.

DIDGERIDOO AND A
GOLD MEDAL, TOO

After Ms. Fitt's class, the Tardy Boys and
Al-Ian walked down the hall toward the
music room.

"I never knew that global warming was
a myth started by companies that make
wind turbines and high-energy batteries
for electric cars," said Leyton.

Al-Ian pointed out a hallway window.
"Look, they've turned on the lawn

sprinklers and kids are running around under them."

"Sure is strange weather for February," said Wade. "I wonder what's causing it to be so warm?"

"According to that video from the National Association of Coal and Oil Distributors, it's just natural temperature variation," said Leyton.

They got to the music room. Al-Ian found a trombone, and Leyton found a zydeco washboard. Wade found a didgeridoo, an instrument made from a hollow tree branch and invented by Australian Aborigines who knew better than to swim in waters infested by box jellyfish.

From there, they went to the rear entrance to the skating rink, which was located at the end of a hall nobody ever went down because it ended at a door that had been locked forever.

"What are we doing here?" asked Al-Ian.

"This is where Daisy told us to meet her," Wade said.

A moment later, Daisy hurried down the hall carrying a wrinkled brown paper bag. "Okay, guys, Olga's going to be here any second. So listen up." She quickly told them her plan.

A few minutes later, Olga arrived pushing her new thirty-six-inch Thunderwear®™ Power Push Sweet Sweep Fine Bristle Push Broom. She had a huge smile on her face. "This is the happiest day of my life!"

"We're so glad for you, Olga," said Wade.

Olga looked around. "Where should I stand?"

"Right here is fine," said Wade.

"Should I take off my silver medal?" Olga asked.

"Definitely," said Daisy. "According to the rules of the International Custodial Olympics, a medal winner must not wear any other medals, metals, or missiles when receiving an award."

"I don't have any missiles," Olga said as she took off her silver medal, "but I do have a metal key ring."

"Daisy will hold it for you," said Wade.

Olga handed Daisy her key ring. It must have had three hundred keys on it.

"According to tradition, the receiver of the award must keep her eyes closed during the entire ceremony," Wade announced. "The opening of eyes during the awards ceremony may result in the immediate loss of all current and past awards and medals."

"I understand," Olga said, and squeezed her eyes shut.

"In addition, the award recipient may not speak or move during the ceremony," Wade said. "Even if you hear strange or disturbing sounds, you must keep your eyes closed and not speak. Do you understand?"

With her eyes closed, Olga nodded. Wade turned to Leyton and Al-Ian. "Gentlemen, please begin to play the award ceremony music."

Al-Ian began to blow on the trombone even though he had never played one before. Leyton began to rake his fingers up and down the washboard. As soon as the noise started, Daisy hurried to the rear door to the ice rink and started to try all the keys on Olga's key ring.

Meanwhile, Wade reached into the

wrinkled paper bag and took out a new tuna fish can top. This one was painted gold and was on a gold ribbon.

"Olga Shotput, it is my great honor to bestow upon you the gold medal for custodianship," Wade said. "You have been deemed worthy of this award after many years of outstanding service in the fields of custodianship and janitoristics."

Meanwhile, Daisy quickly tried key after key in the rear door to the ice rink. Wade glanced at her to see if she'd found the right key. Daisy shook her head and kept trying. Wade turned again to Olga. He had to keep talking until Daisy found the right key.

"This is truly a very great honor," he said while Leyton and Al-Ian continued to make noise on the washboard and trombone. "It is such a great honor that very few other janitors have ever received it. I can probably count on one hand all the janitors who have won it. There aren't many, that's for sure. Hardly any. I bet not a single person in this school can name one."

Al-Ian's face was turning red from blowing on the trombone. Leyton's fingers began to hurt from raking the hard metal washboard. With her eyes squeezed shut and her lips pressed together Olga waited for Wade to put the gold medal of custodianship around her neck. Daisy was still frantically trying the keys but had not yet found the right one.

"Like I was saying," Wade went on. "This is an amazing honor. One of the greatest honors ever. Right up there with the Medal of Honor and the time Connor fell on her. And it's a good thing she wasn't hurt because Connor was a big guy. I guess you could call that one the Medal of On Her. Which I'm about to bestow on her."

Olga balled her hands into fists and squirmed eagerly. Al-Ian was gasping between each toot of the trombone. Leyton put down the washboard and began blowing on the didgeridoo. But Daisy still hadn't found the key to the ice rink's rear entrance.

"And I'd just like to point out that this is indeed the gold medal, not the silver," Wade went on. "Some people may think there's not much difference, but I can tell you there is. When was the last time you saw a silver-medal winner on a box of Wheaties? Silver just isn't in the same league as gold. And forget about bronze. The only reason there are bronze medals is because no one knows what else to do with the stuff. I mean, who can name one other thing that's made of bronze besides bronze medals?"

"Bells, cymbals, and saxophones," said Al-Ian, who'd given up playing the trombone. "And many precision ball bearings."

By now, Olga was so eager to get her medal she was jumping up and down with her eyes squeezed shut and her lips pressed together. Wade glanced at Daisy, who was still racing to find the key to the rear ice rink door.

"Right," Wade said. "Like who really cares about precision ball bearings?"

"Small electric motors do," said Al-Ian.

"Good for them." Wade said. He couldn't think of anything more to say about the gold medal, but if he gave it to Olga she'd open her eyes and see that Daisy was trying to unlock the rear door to the skating rink. He looked at Al-Ian and Leyton. Both of them understood the problem, but they shrugged as if they didn't know how to help. Wade had no choice. He couldn't think of anymore ways to stall. He had to give Olga the medal.

FINALLY, A GOLD-MEDAL-WINNING CUSTODIAN

Leyton could see that his brother was in a jam. But not the kind of jam that is made with whole fruit, cut into pieces or crushed, and then heated with water and sugar. This was a different jam. This was the kind of jam where someone finds himself in a difficult or embarrassing situation. Leyton did not like seeing his brother in that kind of jam, or, for that matter, being heated in water with crushed fruit, either.

Leyton knew that to help get Wade out of the jam, he would have to think. And thinking meant exercising his brain cells, so he concentrated really hard on all those little cells doing push-ups and bench presses and working out on stationary climbers and treadmills. It wasn't easy to imagine because he was pretty sure that brain cells didn't have teeny-tiny legs and arms to do that stuff with.

But then, quite suddenly and without any warning whatsoever, Leyton had an idea! He hurried to Wade and whispered in his ear.

Wade turned to Olga, who was still jumping up and down with her eyes shut and her lips pressed closed, but had now turned bright red. "Olga Shotput, are you ready for your gold medal?"

Olga nodded eagerly.

"Then there is just one last question I must ask," said Wade. "If I give you the gold medal in custodianship, will you show Daisy which key opens the rear door to the ice rink?"

Olga stopped hopping up and down. Her forehead wrinkled and her lips bunched with frustration. She pointed at her mouth and made some strange noises.

"I think she needs to speak," said Al-Ian.

"I see," said Wade. "All right. I will make an exception to the rules of the International Custodial Olympics and allow you to speak."

"Thank you," said Olga. "I would like to show Daisy which key unlocks the door, but I promised Assistant Principal Snout that I would never let any student use my keys."

"Is that the same assistant principal who gave you that stupid thirty-six-inch Thunderwear®™ Power Push Sweet Sweep Fine Bristle Push Broom when what you really wanted was a gold medal for custodianship?" asked Wade.

Olga thought for a moment. "True that," she said.

"Excellent," said Wade. "You may show Daisy which key opens the door and then return here for the completion of the gold medal ceremony."

Olga showed Daisy which key opened the rear door to the skating rink and then returned to receive her gold medal. As Wade held it up he caught a glimpse of his reflection in the gold paint. His hair

was sticking out every which way. If there had been a gold medal for unruly hair, Wade was certain he would win it.

A few moments later, Olga left, pushing her brand new thirty-six-inch Thunderwear®™ Power Push Sweet Sweep Fine Bristle Push Broom. Once again tears poured out of her eyes.

But these were tears of joy. She was now, finally, a gold-medal–winning custodian!

Leyton went over to his brother and put his hand on his shoulder. "I'm proud of you, dude."

"All I did was give her a fake gold medal," Wade said.

"Yeah, but did you see how happy it made her?" Leyton asked.

Wade did see how happy Olga was. He wondered what it would take to make

him that happy. And there was only one answer — a cure for CUHS.

A moment later, Daisy came back out through the rear door to the ice rink. "It's just as I suspected," she said and started to jog away down the hall.

"What's just as you suspected?" Wade asked, following her.

"Where are you going?" asked Al-Ian as he, too, followed.

Daisy didn't answer. They trailed her all the way back to Assistant Principal Snout's office. Daisy hurried in and quickly washed her hands and kicked off her shoes. A few moments later, Daisy, the Tardy Boys, and Al-Ian were once again sitting in the assistant principal's office. On the other side of the bullet- and soundproof glass Assistant Principal Snout watched the all-news channel.

"You're making a mistake," Daisy said.

Assistant Principal Snout pointed at his ear and shook his head. Then he picked up the phone. The Tardy Boys and their friends reached for the telephone receivers on the wall behind them.

"What are you doing here?" asked Assistant Principal Snout.

"Those creatures in the skating rink aren't small, flightless black-and-white aliens," Daisy said. "They're penguins."

"That's impossible," replied Assistant Principal Snout. "There are no penguins in the Northern Hemisphere."

"Have you seen them yourself?" Daisy asked.

"Yes," answered the assistant principal.

"Of all the creatures you have seen on Earth, which did they most resemble?" Daisy asked.

"Without a doubt, they look almost exactly like penguins," said Assistant Principal Snout.

"That's because they *are* penguins," Daisy insisted.

Assistant Principal Snout calmly shook his head. "Not possible. We are at least two thousand miles from the nearest natural penguin habitat."

"So?" said Daisy.

"So if they were penguins, how did they get here?" asked Assistant Principal Snout.

"Haven't you heard of *The March of the Penguins*?" asked Leyton.

"That's a long way to march," said Assistant Principal Snout.

"Maybe they hitched a ride on an iceberg," said Daisy. "All I know is they're not aliens. They're penguins."

Once again, Assistant Principal Snout shook his head. "I'm sorry, but that's impossible."

Meanwhile, the scene on the HDTV switched to a reporter with long red hair standing in front of a large outdoor skating rink. Behind her, adults and children were hurrying out of a doorway as if they were being chased off the ice. The camera then moved closer to the ice rink where dozens of penguins could be seen flapping their flippers and chasing skaters.

"Do you realize that in all of history there has never been a single recorded instance of a penguin finding its way on its own into the Northern Hemisphere?" asked Assistant Principal Snout. "Not unless it was brought here by human beings."

On the HDTV the scene switched to the famous ice rink at Rockefeller Center in New York where penguins were chasing people off the ice. And from there, it switched to a scene at yet another ice rink where penguins were pecking angrily at anyone who tried to enter.

"So, I'm sorry, Daisy," said Assistant Principal Snout. "I know you'd like to think they're penguins. But they're obviously visitors from another planet."

By now, the Tardy Boys and their friends were all pointing at the HDTV. Assistant Principal Snout turned to look. The scene had switched to a newsroom where a news anchor was speaking to the camera. Behind him were a dozen different scenes of penguins in ice rinks. Assistant Principal Snout's mouth fell open. He reached forward and turned up the sound.

"While no one has been able to communicate with the penguins to find out exactly what they want," the anchor was saying, "scientists believe that it has something to do with global warming and the melting of their native habitats."

Assistant Principal Snout turned to the Tardy Boys and their friends and said, "Shouldn't you kids be in class?"

THE HEAVILY ARMED PENGUIN PROTECTION COMMANDOS

Out in the hall, Leyton said, "So they really are penguins."

"I'm still not so sure." said Al-Ian.

"Why not?" asked Wade.

"They looked awful small," said Al-Ian.

"Not all penguins are big like the emperor penguin," said Daisy. "Some only weigh two or three pounds."

"And I read that they don't all live in

Antarctica," said Wade. "Don't some live in warm climates?"

"True that, Wade," said Daisy. "Some even live in the Galápagos Islands, which are right on the equator. It can get as warm as ninety degrees there and never goes below sixty."

"That's like around here these days," said Al-Ian. "I mean, look outside. It's the middle of February, and there are bees going from flower to flower."

The others stopped to gaze out the windows and admire the buzzing bees. Then Leyton looked past them and noticed that something was the same, but something was also different about the SWAT team surrounding the ice rink.

The same: They were still wearing helmets and body armor.

Different: Their uniforms were no longer dark blue. They were now light green.

"Why did the SWAT team change its uniform?" Leyton asked.

"Because it was feeling blue?" Al-Ian guessed.

"Because they weren't *agreen* on what to wear?" guessed Wade.

"Because it wanted to be a SWAMP team?" guessed Daisy.

"It's not a riddle," Leyton said. "They really did change their uniforms."

Wade and the others stared at the heavily armed men and women guarding the ice rink.

"I don't think that's a police SWAT team anymore," said Wade.

"Then what kind of SWAT team is it?" asked Al-Ian.

"Let's find out," said Daisy. She and the others went outside and walked over to the closest heavily-armed person. This was a tall, broad-shouldered woman with a dark ponytail. She was wearing mirrored sunglasses. Her face was painted with green-and-black camoflauge makeup. On her green uniform were the letters HAPPCO.

"Stop!" The woman held out a black-gloved hand. "Don't come any closer."

"Who are you?" Daisy asked.

"I am Sergeant N. Dangered and I am the commander of the Heavily Armed Penguin Protection Commandos," the woman said.

"You're here to protect the penguins?" Wade asked.

"Yes, sir."

"Why did the SWAT team leave?" asked Leyton.

"Uh . . ." Sergeant N. Dangered thought hard. "Because it had somewhere else to go? No, no, wait. Uh . . . because it wanted to be a SWENT team? No, wait! Uh . . . because . . ."

"It's not a riddle," Leyton said. "I was just asking why they left."

"Oh." Sergeant N. Dangered's shoulders sagged with disappointment. "Because penguins took over the ice rink, not aliens."

"Why do you need to be heavily armed to protect penguins?" Daisy asked.

"We don't want any harm to come to them," answered Sergeant N. Dangered.

"Wait a minute," said Al-Ian. "You'd hurt someone if you thought he was going to harm a penguin?"

"That is correct," said Sergeant N. Dangered.

"But then you'd be harming a human," said Leyton.

"Correct," said Sergeant N. Dangered.

"So, you'd harm a human, but not a penguin?" asked Daisy.

"Absolutely," said Sergeant N. Dangered.

"That doesn't make sense," said Wade.

"Maybe not, but those are my orders," said Sergeant N. Dangered.

THE GREAT AUK

By now, it was time for their next class. The Tardy Boys and their friends went back into school and returned to Ms. Fitt's room.

"What subject is this?" Ms. Fitt asked after the students were seated.

"Math," said Wade.

Ms. Fitt picked up the TV remote and began flipping through the channels. "Let's see what we can find that relates to math." She stopped at a channel where a woman was selling a necklace. "Perfect! We'll watch the jewelry shopping channel."

"How will that teach us math?" asked Wade.

"Because it's about shopping, and you need math in order to shop," Ms. Fitt explained.

Daisy raised her hand. "Ms. Fitt, did you know that those aren't aliens in the ice rink? They're penguins?"

Ms. Fitt frowned. "Why would there be penguins in the ice rink?"

"We think it's because global warming is melting the Antarctic ice cap and destroying the penguins' natural habitat," said Daisy. "So the penguins are taking over human ice rinks to show us what it's like to have our ice taken away."

"So what? asked Fibby Mandible. "Why do you care about those stupid birds anyway?"

"Because it's wrong for us to destroy their natural habitat," Daisy said.

"I disagree," said Barton. "I'm a big fan of extinction. Last night, I went on the Internet and looked up how many different species we've eliminated. You wouldn't believe how many there are. I mean with just birds alone we've gotten rid of the dodo, the passenger pigeon, the great auk, the Labrador duck, and a lot more. So what's the big deal if we add one more to the list?"

"You can't be serious," said Daisy.

"I'm totally serious," said Barton. "Long before humans were here, lots of species of animals went extinct without us. Why should the possible extinction of one of today's species matter?"

"I agree with Barton," said Fibby. "Besides, even if we force penguins into extinction, we'll still be able to see as much of them as we want because we've got all those penguin movies."

"But that's so wrong!" Daisy gasped, and looked toward their teacher. "Ms. Fitt, tell them they're wrong."

But Ms. Fitt wasn't listening. She was standing by the classroom windows, looking outside at the long caravan of TV news vans snaking through the school's entrance and parking around the ice rink. Cameramen were setting up cameras on tripods and reporters were taking out microphones.

"The media's here," she said.

The class left their seats and joined Ms. Fitt at the window. By now, the reporters were facing the cameras. Ms. Fitt hurried over to her desk, picked up the remote, and changed the TV channel. On the screen, the class saw a reporter speaking with The School With No Name's ice rink behind her.

"This is Lucy Lipps with the KWAK Instant News Team," said the reporter. "I'm here at The School With No Name where officials say they're at a standoff with the penguins that have taken over the skating rink. The penguins refuse to leave the ice, and school officials can't make them. Here with us to discuss the problem is Assistant Principal Snout."

The camera panned over to Assistant Principal Snout, who was wearing his yellow earplugs, white breathing mask, and blue latex gloves.

"Sir, can you tell us what you plan to do about the penguins?" asked Ms. Lipps.

Assistant Principal Snout looked at the camera. "Am I really on TV?"

"Yes, sir," said Ms. Lipps. "Now, if you'd just answer my question."

"How do I look?" asked Assistant Principal Snout.

"Uh, except for the earplugs, breathing mask, and latex gloves, I'd say you look just fine," said Ms. Lipps. "Now, if you wouldn't mind answering the question."

Assistant Principal Snout waved a blue latex glove. "Hi, Mom!"

"Sir, if you can't stay on topic I'm afraid I'm going to have to end this interview," Ms. Lipps warned. "Now once again, can you tell us what you plan to do about the penguins?"

"Oh, sorry," said Assistant Principal Snout. "Uh, we don't really have a plan for the penguins. Frankly I'd like to pluck their feathers and make penguin pajamas, but all these annoying animal rights and environmental groups won't let me."

"But you must have some idea of what you're going to do," said Ms. Lipps.

"Not really," said Assistant Principal Snout. "Mostly we just hope someone comes along and saves us. What we need right now is a hero. Someone who'll take charge and lead us out of this terrible mess."

Ms. Lipps turned to the camera. "You heard it here first, folks. Administrators at The School With No Name are looking for a hero. And whoever that hero turns out to be, we at KWAK guarantee you'll see him or her here first."

The TV cut back to the KWAK newsroom, and Ms. Fitt turned off the sound.

"Looks like we need a hero," she said while the students returned to their seats.

"And whoever it is will get to be on KWAK," said Barton.

"That's right," said Ms. Fitt. "This is a chance for one of you to appear on national TV."

A CHAPTER HEADING THAT HAS NOTHING TO DO WITH THIS BOOK

The Tardy Boys and their friends spent the rest of the period watching the jewelry shopping channel. By the end of the period, they hadn't learned much about math, but they did know that a white crystal rhinestone necklace for $125 was an excellent value and would sell quickly.

"I'm thinking about getting that diamond superhero earring," said Leyton.

"But you don't have a pierced ear," said Al-Ian.

"Doesn't matter," said Leyton. "Did you see the price? How could you not buy it?"

"We have to find out what the penguins want," Daisy said.

"What do you mean?" asked Al-Ian.

"There's a reason they're taking over ice rinks around the world," said Daisy. "And we have to figure out what it is."

"I thought it was because they're angry that Antarctica is melting," said Wade.

"I think there may be more to it than that," said Daisy. "It's hard to imagine that they really want to spend the rest of their lives on an ice rink."

"True that," said Al-Ian. "But how do we find out what they want?"

"We'll have to talk to them," Daisy said.

"Uh, I have news for you, Daisy," said Leyton. "Penguins don't speak English."

"Right," said Daisy. "So we'll have to learn to speak Penguin."

"How?" asked Leyton. "I know they teach French and Spanish in this school, but I've never heard of anyone talking Penguin."

"Then we'll have to teach ourselves," said Daisy, and started down the hall.

"Where are you going?" asked Wade.

"To the library," said Daisy.

Leyton and Wade couldn't go to the library with Daisy because they had gym. They went to their lockers and got their hockey bags, and then went to the gym. But when they got to the gym, all the kids were standing around in their regular clothes.

"What's going on?" Wade asked Al-Ian.

"We can't play hockey because the penguins have taken over the ice rink," said Al-Ian. "So Mr. Braun is trying to figure out what we should do instead."

Mr. Braun was the new gym teacher. He had dark hair and muscles on top of muscles. He had so many muscles that they stretched his polo shirt tight, so many muscles that he even had muscles inside his skull where his brain was supposed to be. There was a rumor that Mr. Braun had been the gym teacher over in Jeffersonville, but that he'd left because of a kid named Barry Dunn.

The door to the gym office opened, and Mr. Braun came out pulling a cart with a big TV strapped to it. "Okay, runts, settle down!" he shouted. "Get comfortable on the floor. You're gonna watch a hockey movie."

Wade raised his hand.

"What is it, Tardy?" asked Mr. Braun, who called everyone by their last name when he wasn't calling them runts.

"Can't we go outside?" Wade asked.

Mr. Braun shook his massive head. "Are you nuts, Tardy? It's the middle of winter."

"But it's a beautiful eighty-degree day," Wade said. "Kids are running under lawn sprinklers and the butterflies are fluttering by."

"Mr. Circle, our old gym teacher, used to send us out when there was six feet of snow on the ground," said Leyton.

"Okay, and where's Mr. Circle today?" asked Mr. Braun.

"We don't know," said Al-Ian. "One day he disappeared, and the next day you became our gym teacher."

"That's because he got fired for making you runts go out in the snow," said Mr. Braun. "So I don't care what it's like outside. As long as it's winter, you're staying in here."

Some of the kids in class groaned because they wanted to go outside. Others just shrugged and sat down. Mr. Braun fiddled with the TV and the remote. He appeared to be having a problem getting it to play. The TV screen was all gray snow.

"What are we gonna watch?" someone asked.

"If you don't quiet down you won't get to watch anything," warned Mr. Braun, still clicking the remote without success. "One of you runts want to help me get this thing to work?"

"I will!" Al-Ian volunteered and took the

remote from Mr. Braun. He got the TV to go on and started flipping through the channels, passing one where Wade thought he caught a glimpse of something familiar.

"Go back!" Wade said.

Al-Ian flipped back. The next thing the gym class knew, they were watching Fibby and Barton on TV being interviewed by Lucy Lipps of KWAK.

"You said your name is Fibby Mandible and you're the executive director of Save the Penguins?" Ms. Lipps asked.

"Yes," Fibby said. "These poor penguins have been displaced from their homes. They need food. I've ordered my mother to get all the fish she can find for them."

"That's so nice of you," said Ms. Lipps.

"I know," said Fibby. "And in honor of the penguins, I have created an interpretive ice dance called Small and Flightless and Free, which I will debut tonight during the auditions for *American Super Mega Idol Star Search*. I hope all your viewers will tune in and vote for me, Fibby Mandible, America's next Super Mega Idol Star."

"Uh, well, I certainly hope so, too," Ms. Lipps said and turned to Barton. "And you are?"

"Barton Slugg, senior vice president in charge of comedy for Save the Penguins," Barton said.

"And what exactly do you do?" Ms. Lipps asked.

"Well, Ms. Lipps," Barton said, "as I'm sure you can imagine, these penguins are very upset by what's happened to them. They need to have their spirits lifted. That's where I come in."

"By telling them jokes?" Ms. Lipps asked uncertainly.

"Not just any jokes," said Barton. "Penguin jokes. For instance, 'What's black and white and goes around and around?'"

"I have no idea," said the reporter.

"A penguin in a revolving door."

"That's not funny," said Ms. Lipps. She started to turn away, but Barton grabbed the microphone and turned to face the camera.

"How about this one?" Barton said. "Why do penguins carry fish in their beaks? Because they don't have any pockets."

Ms. Lipps tried to pull the microphone back, but Barton wouldn't let go.

"Just remember," Barton said, "a vote for me is a vote for penguins everywhere.

Tune in tonight for more of my great penguin jokes on *American Super Mega Idol Star Search*."

Ms. Lipps tore the microphone from Barton's grasp. "And that was Barton Slugg, senior vice president in charge of comedy for Save the Penguins. Now back to you, Bob."

"Ahem!" Mr. Braun cleared his throat.

Al-Ian switched over to the hockey movie that his gym teacher had chosen. Wade leaned toward Leyton and whispered, "Fibby and Barton don't give a hoot about the penguins. They're just trying to get people to watch them tonight on *American Super Mega Idol Star Search*."

"What should we do?" Leyton asked.

"As soon as gym is over, we have to tell Daisy," said Wade.

A CURE FOR CUHS

When gym was over, the Tardy Boys lugged their hockey bags back to their lockers.

"I can't believe we carried these bags all the way to school today and didn't even have hockey," Wade complained.

"True, but carrying heavy things is good exercise and helps build muscle," said Leyton.

Wade doubted that. Carrying heavy things might have helped his brother build big muscles, but Wade was certain he would always be scrawny no matter how much weight he lifted. And he would always suffer from Chronic Unruly Hair Syndrome. It just wasn't fair.

After putting their hockey bags in their lockers, the Tardy Boys went to the library, where they found Al-Ian telling Daisy how Fibby and Barton had pretended on TV that they cared about the penguins. Sitting at a computer, Daisy listened to what Al-Ian said.

"Why aren't I surprised?" she grumbled when Al-Ian had finished.

"What are we going to do?" asked Al-Ian.

"We're not going to worry about Fibby and Barton," Daisy said. "We're going to concentrate on helping the penguins by communicating with them and finding out what they want."

"Have you figured out how penguins communicate?" asked Al-Ian.

"Not entirely," said Daisy. "What I do know is that each species of penguin has its own voice or call. Each penguin has its own particular sound. Penguins can recognize one another by their voices. Penguins also communicate by staring, bowing, paddling, pecking, bumping, and crouching."

"Does that mean you want us to stare, bow, paddle, peck, bump, and crouch with penguins?" Wade asked.

"It might be our only chance," said Daisy.

"How about we do the staring, bowing,

and paddling and you do the pecking, bumping, and crouching?" Leyton asked.

"Hey, guys, look at that." Al-Ian pointed at the library windows. Outside, a large black tanker truck had pulled up beside the ice rink. On the side of the truck, in big white letters, was:

THUNDERWEAR®™ PENGUIN OIL COMPANY

"What's penguin oil?" Leyton asked.

"Whoa, look who just got out of the truck," said Wade.

It was Ulna Mandible. A moment later, Fibby ran up to her and started to wave her arms and yell.

"What's she saying?" Daisy asked.

Al-Ian opened the window and they crowded around to listen.

"Why did you come in that truck?" Fibby yelled at her mom.

"You said you wanted me to get all the fish I could find," Ulna answered.

"But why couldn't you bring them in the Hummer?" said Fibby.

"Because they'd die without water," said Ulna.

Fibby stared at the tanker truck. "You got *live* fish?"

"Isn't that what you wanted?" asked Ulna.

"No!" Fibby screeched. "I wanted dead fish. Dead, but *fresh!* To feed the penguins."

Ulna put her hands on her hips. "Well, you should have *said* so."

"Well, I'm saying so now," Fibby yelled. "Go get me fresh dead fish. And whatever you do, don't bring them back in this truck."

Ulna got back into the Thunderwear®™ Penguin Oil Company tanker truck and raced out of the school parking lot.

"Why didn't Fibby want anyone to see that truck?" Leyton asked.

"It must have something to do with what penguin oil is," said Wade, heading over to one of the computers. In the reflection of the screen, he saw his hair poking away from his head like an octopus's tentacles. *Don't despair just because you have unruly hair,* he thought. He typed in penguin oil and studied the results. "Uh-oh."

"What is it?" Daisy asked.

"I don't think you want to see this," Wade said.

"Why not?" asked Daisy.

Wade stepped aside and let Daisy read what he'd found. Daisy quickly studied the screen. "Oh, no!" she gasped. "The only way to get penguin oil from penguins is by cooking them!"

"That's not the only bad news," said Al-Ian, who was sitting at another computer. "I just looked up the Thunderwear®™ Penguin Oil Company. And guess what? It's owned by Sternum Mandible!"

"Fibby's father!" Daisy gasped.

"That means that Fibby doesn't want to save the penguins at all," Wade realized. "She's just pretending. What she really wants to do is get them for her father's penguin oil company."

"But why would anyone want penguin oil?" asked Al-Ian.

Wade read down the website to see what the uses of penguin oil were. It was mostly used in cosmetics and hair care products. His eyes widened when he reached the line that said:

> In addition to its other benefits, penguin oil is the only known remedy for CUHS, otherwise known as Chronic Unruly Hair Syndrome.

Wade stared at the computer screen in disbelief. Was it really true? Had he finally found the answer to his problems? "I can't believe it," he gasped.

"Can't believe what?" asked Daisy.

"Oh, nothing," Wade replied, and quickly closed the website before anyone else could see.

WHACK JOBS

"We have to save those penguins before Fibby's father gets them," Daisy said, and started out of the library.

"Does that mean we're going to stare, bow, paddle, peck, bump, and crouch?" Leyton asked as he and the others followed.

"There's another way that penguins

communicate," said Daisy. "They flap their wings."

"Penguins have wings?" said Al-Ian.

"Not really," Daisy said, hurrying down the hall.

"Then how do they communicate by flapping wings they don't have?" asked Leyton.

"By using their flippers," said Daisy.

The Tardy Boys and Al-Ian shared puzzled looks.

"Listen," Daisy said over her shoulder. "It doesn't matter what you call them. The point is, that's how we can communicate with them."

"By flapping the wings we don't have?" asked Al-Ian.

"Or flapping the flippers we don't have?" asked Wade.

"Watch," said Daisy. She stuck her thumbs in her armpits and then flapped her elbows.

"You have to be kidding me," said Wade. "You expect me to do *that*?"

"Why not?" asked Daisy.

"Because I'll look like a whack job," said Wade.

"True that," said Daisy. "But no one will see you looking like a whack job because we'll be the only ones in the ice rink."

"*You'll* see me looking like a whack job," said Wade. Then he turned to his brother and Al-Ian. "And they will, too."

"I don't think looking like a whack job is so bad," said Leyton.

"That's because you're so good-looking that you couldn't look like a whack job if you tried," said Wade. "But with my unruly hair, I sometimes look like a whack job even when I don't mean to."

Daisy stopped. "Suppose Al-Ian and I also look like whack jobs? And suppose Leyton at least *tries* to look like a whack job? Would that make you feel better?"

"I'm not sure," said Wade. "I guess. Maybe. I'd have to see."

Daisy turned to Al-Ian and Leyton. "Okay, guys, let's all try to look like whack jobs."

Al-Ian crossed his eyes, puckered his lips, and put his thumbs in his ears. Leyton slid his pinkies into his nostrils and stuck out his tongue.

Daisy stared at them. "What are you guys doing?"

"You said we should try to look like whack jobs," Leyton said.

"By sticking your thumbs in your armpits and flapping your elbows," Daisy said.

"Oh." Leyton turned to Al-Ian. "Did you know that?"

Al-Ian shook his head.

Daisy stuck her thumbs in her armpits. "Let's give it a try."

The Tardy Boys and Al-Ian stuck their thumbs in their armpits.

"One, two, three, flap!" Daisy said.

Everyone flapped their elbows.

Just then, Assistant Principal Snout and Mr. Braun, the gym teacher, came around the corner.

I'M DREAMING OF A TROPICAL CHRISTMAS

"What are you doing?" asked Assistant Principal Snout.

The Tardy Boys and their friends pulled their thumbs out of their armpits and shared embarrassed looks.

"Uh, we were exercising," said Wade.

"You're not supposed to exercise in the hall," said Assistant Principal Snout. "You're supposed to exercise in gym."

"But all we do in gym is watch movies," said Al-Ian.

Assistant Principal Snout turned to Mr. Braun. "Is that true?"

"They were supposed to be in the ice rink for hockey, but those birds took it over," said Mr. Braun. "So we watched a hockey movie in the gym instead."

"We could have played basketball or indoor soccer," said Leyton.

"Not if you were scheduled for hockey," said Mr. Braun.

"That's right," said Assistant Principal Snout. "There'll be no playing basketball or indoor soccer when you're scheduled for hockey." He turned to Mr. Braun. "Now what were we talking about before these students so rudely interrupted us?"

"Changing the schedule," said Mr. Braun.

"Ah, yes," said Assistant Principal Snout

as he and the gym teacher started to walk away. "And what were you saying?"

"I think that as long as it's this warm out we might want to take the students outside instead of keeping them inside," said Mr. Braun.

"And what would they do?" asked Assistant Principal Snout.

"They could play soccer or basketball," said Mr. Braun.

The Tardy Boys and their friends watched as the assistant principal and gym teacher disappeared around a corner.

"Did that make sense to anyone?" asked Wade.

"About as much sense as doing this," Al-Ian said, sticking his thumbs in his armpits and flapping his elbows.

"That makes perfect sense," said Daisy, "if you're a penguin."

"But I'm not a penguin and that's what I don't understand," Al-Ian said. "We flapped our elbows, but what did we say?"

"Don't worry," said Daisy. "The penguins will know."

Using the key, Daisy opened the rear entrance to the skating rink. They all went in. The air felt chilly, and goose bumps ran up and down Leyton's arms. As they walked around the stands toward the ice, they could hear lots of penguin chatter.

A moment later they saw the penguins. The ice rink was filled with them. Like Al-Ian said, they weren't the biggest penguins in the world. They were all standing around like they were waiting for a train. A few were bowing, and here and there one was bumping and crouching. Most were staring over the ice rink wall — at Daisy, Al-Ian, and the Tardy Boys.

"Whoa," said Wade. "They look sort of blue."

"Wait a minute," said Al-Ian. "They *are* sort of blue!"

This was true. The penguin's heads were covered with bluish feathers.

"They also don't look very happy," said Leyton.

"Why should they?" Daisy asked. "Thanks to global warming, they've lost their native habitat."

"That's not true," said Leyton. "According to the video from National Association of Coal and Oil Distributors, the warming of the planet is simply natural temperature variation. That's why it's the middle of February and eighty-five degrees outside."

"Leyton, that video was made by people who sell oil and coal," Daisy said. "They'll say anything to try to make you believe that global warming has nothing to do with greenhouse gases, because burning oil and coal are two of the biggest producers of greenhouse gases."

"But how do you know they're wrong about natural temperature variations?" Leyton asked.

"Leyton, how many Christmas songs do you know?" Daisy asked.

"A bunch," Leyton said.

"And have you ever heard a single one where they talk about wearing bathing suits? Or going swimming? Or picking flowers?" Daisy asked.

Wade turned to Leyton. "She's got a good point."

Meanwhile, a group of penguins were waddling across the ice toward them. Leading them was a male penguin that was slightly taller than the others. He had a small dark blue spot on his white chest. The other penguins were careful to stay a step behind him.

"Something tells me he's their leader," Al-Ian whispered.

"Who wants to try to talk to him?" Daisy asked.

"Why don't you?" said Wade.

Daisy pushed open the low gate in the ice rink wall and stepped out onto the ice. She stuck her thumbs into her armpits and flapped her elbows. The penguins cocked their heads and looked puzzled. Daisy looked back at the boys. "Maybe one of you should try."

Al-Ian and Wade both went through the gate and out onto the ice where they flapped their elbows. But the penguins still looked puzzled.

"It's not working," Wade said.

Daisy turned to Leyton. "You're the only one who hasn't tried."

"If they don't understand you guys, why would they understand me?" Leyton asked.

"Maybe you could try something different," Daisy suggested.

Leyton went through the gate and out onto the ice. He had no idea what to do so he told the cells in his skull to start exercising. The brain cells did sit-ups and squats and climbed ropes. Suddenly, Leyton had an idea. He flapped his elbows like the others had, but then he spun around on the ice and bowed.

Suddenly, the penguins behind the leader started to squawk excitedly.

"It worked!" Daisy gasped. "Do it again!"

Leyton flapped, spun, and bowed again. The penguins behind the leader squawked louder and more excitedly. Suddenly, the leader turned and screeched angrily at them. All the other penguins quickly quieted. Then the leader turned to Leyton and screeched and flapped angrily.

"Whoa, he is one ticked-off penguin," Al-Ian said.

"What should I do?" Leyton asked.

"Try flapping your elbows, then bow, then spin around, then shake your head."

Leyton did as he was told.

The penguins behind the leader went bonkers, squawking and flapping and shaking their heads back and forth. The leader turned and screeched loudly at them, but it was no use. All the penguins started to waddle around him.

They were heading straight for Leyton!

THE ATTACK OF THE LITTLE BLUE PENGUINS

"Get out of there, Leyton!" Wade shouted.

Leyton tried to run toward the gate in the rink wall, but his feet slipped out from beneath him and he fell. Lying on the hard, cold ice, he looked back over his shoulder. A mass of penguins was scuttling toward him!

"Hurry, Leyton!" Daisy cried.

Leyton got to his feet, then slipped again. The penguins were coming closer. "Help!" he yelled.

The others scurried through the gate and pulled him off the ice, slamming the gate closed behind them. They huddled together on the concrete on the other side of the ice rink wall and caught their breaths.

"What'd I say?" Leyton gasped.

"I don't know," said Daisy, "but it sure got those other penguins mad."

"Especially the leader," said Wade. "I don't think I've ever seen a more annoyed penguin."

"Uh, guys?" Al-Ian said.

"Just a minute, Al-Ian," Daisy said. "Listen, if we can figure out what Leyton said to them, then we can figure out how to communicate."

"As long as we don't say the same thing Leyton just said," said Wade, reminding them.

"Guys?" Al-Ian said.

"Not now, Al-Ian," said Daisy. "We have to figure out what Leyton said that made the penguins so excited."

"I think it had to do with the bowing part," said Wade.

"Uh, guys?" said Al-Ian.

"Just wait, Al-Ian," said Daisy. "I think it had more to do with Leyton shaking his head."

"Uh, guys?" Al-Ian said. "I really hate to interrupt..."

Daisy turned to him and asked impatiently, "What is it?"

Al-Ian pointed at the skating rink. The gate was closed, but on the other side the small penguins were climbing up on one another's backs. Those penguins that reached the top of the pile stood on the gate for a moment and then hopped down onto the concrete floor on the other side.

And headed straight for Leyton!

SERIOUSLY TICKED OFF

The Tardy Boys and their friends stared
in disbelief at the growing crowd of
penguins crawling over the gate and
waddling toward them, flapping their
flippers and squawking excitedly.

Wade swallowed nervously. "Does
anyone beside me get the feeling that it's
time to run?"

The Tardy Boys and their friends dashed through the ice rink door and out into the hall. Daisy was the last one out, and she made sure the door was closed behind her. Everyone stopped in the hall and huddled together once again while they caught their breaths.

"I don't know what you said to those penguins," Wade said to Leyton. "But it seriously ticked them off. If you hadn't gotten out of there, I hate to think of what might have happened to you."

"Uh, guys?"Al-Ian said.

"Not now, Al-Ian," said Daisy. "Leyton, try to remember when the penguins first started to get excited."

Leyton tried to remember. The brain cells in his head did jumping jacks and cartwheels.

"Uh, guys," said Al-Ian.

"Al-Ian, please!" Daisy said. "Can't you see that Leyton is trying to think?"

"I think it may have been when I spun around," Leyton said.

"Guys?" Al-Ian said.

"I said not now, Al-Ian," said Daisy and turned to Leyton. "Do you remember what you did next?"

"I think I bowed," said Leyton.

"Ahem!" Al-Ian cleared his throat loudly and nodded his head at the rear door of the ice rink. The others looked. The door was starting to open.

"I thought you locked it," Wade said to Daisy.

"I closed it," Daisy said. "It doesn't lock from the inside."

By now more than a dozen penguins had squeezed through the doorway and out into the hall. More were spilling out behind them. At first, they looked around and seemed puzzled to find themselves in a school hallway, but then one of them spotted Leyton.

A second later, they were all squawking and flapping and waddling toward Leyton as fast as they could.

"Run!" Wade cried.

A COLONY, A PARCEL,
OR A HUDDLE

The Tardy Boys and their friends ran to
the nearest room, which just happened
to be Ms. Fitt's. Inside, Ms. Fitt was busy
answering e-mails while her class
watched a video called *Why Watching
Television Is Safer Than Going Outside*,
produced by the American Association of
Couch Manufacturers.

Inside the room, the Tardy Boys shoved empty desks against the door and pressed their weight against them.

Ms. Fitt looked up from her computer. "Is something wrong?"

"We're being chased by a herd of angry penguins," Leyton gasped.

"I don't think it would be a herd," said Barton Slugg, who was in this class. "I think it would be a flock, like other birds."

"Not all birds are in flocks," said Al-Ian. "Geese form a gaggle."

"Actually, geese can be in either a gaggle or a flock," said Ms. Fitt. "But a group of penguins can be called a colony, a parcel, or a huddle."

"They didn't seem like a parcel," said Wade.

"Personally, I wouldn't call them a huddle," said Daisy.

"Can we all agree on a colony?" asked Al-Ian.

"I don't know," said Leyton. "They didn't really strike me as a colony. They're more like an angry mob."

"I'd have to agree with Leyton," said Daisy.

Whomp! Suddenly, there was a loud bang and the door shook.

Ms. Fitt sat up straight. "What in the world was that?"

"If I had to guess," Leyton grunted, "I'd say it was an angry mob, parcel, huddle, or colony of penguins."

The door began to open. Leyton and Wade leaned their weight against the desks piled against the door. But no matter how hard they pushed, the door slowly continued to move.

"Pushing on the door?" Ms. Fitt smiled

and relaxed. "Oh, that's silly. Penguins couldn't push that hard. And besides, why would they want to?"

"That's a good question, Ms. Fitt," Wade groaned as he and Leyton pushed back as hard as they could. "The problem is, we don't know the answer."

"All we know is that Leyton must have said something that really ruffled their feathers," said Daisy.

"Penguins don't have feathers," snorted Fibby.

"Actually, they have short, densely packed feathers," said Ms. Fitt. "But whatever is pushing that door can't be penguins."

"You want to bet?" asked Al-Ian.

Ms. Fitt got up from her computer and came over to the door, which was open just enough for dozens of skinny little black penguin beaks to stick through. Ms. Fitt brought her fingers to her lips. "Oh, dear, there *are* a lot of penguins out there." She turned to Leyton. "What did you say to them?"

"It wasn't exactly words," Leyton said as he struggled to keep the desks pressed against the door. "It was more like sign language."

"Then show us," said Ms. Fitt.

"Do I have to?" Leyton asked, knowing that the other kids would think he looked like a whack job.

"It would be very helpful," said Ms. Fitt.

"How would it be helpful?" asked Daisy, who also did not want Leyton to look like a whack job.

"If you show us what you did, then we'll all know not to do the same thing the next time we're around penguins," said

Ms. Fitt. "That way we won't have to worry about being attacked."

"But how is that going to help us right now?" Wade asked as his feet slowly slid backward and the door gradually opened. Some of the penguins began to stick their heads into the classroom and squawk excitedly.

Ms. Fitt paused and rubbed her chin thoughtfully. "That's a very astute question."

"Is it an astute question because it was asked by an *astudent?*" asked Al-Ian.

By now the penguins were not only able to stick their heads in through the doorway, but a flapping flipper as well. The squawking was growing louder and louder.

Fibby raised her hand. "I'm scared, Ms. Fitt."

"Yeah," said Barton. "I think we have a problem."

"I agree," said Ms. Fitt. "And as you know, a big part of education is learning to solve problems. So how would you solve this?"

A kid in the class raised his hand. "Change the channel?"

"Good suggestion," said Ms. Fitt. "Unfortunately, that will not work here, today."

The Tardy Boys' feet kept sliding back as the penguins pushed harder and harder against the door. By now, some of the penguins were able to get both flippers through the doorway. Wade knew it was only a matter of moments before the penguins burst in.

Barton raised his hand. "I know what

we could do! We could throw Leyton out into the hall."

"Yes," said Ms. Fitt. "Now you're getting closer to a solution."

"Are you serious!?" Leyton gasped.

"Oh, come on, Leyton," said Ms. Fitt. "They're just penguins."

"But there are thousands of them out there!" Leyton said.

"You're exaggerating, Leyton," said Ms. Fitt. "There might be hundreds. Maybe one thousand. But not *thousands*."

"However many there are, they're enough to peck his eyeballs out," Wade cried.

"That's what crows do," Fibby said. "Not penguins."

"Does anyone know which part of the body penguins peck at first?" asked Ms. Fitt.

Meanwhile the door was gradually opening more and more. The penguins were closer and closer to entering the room. Leyton's feet kept sliding backward. It would only be a matter of seconds before the students learned the answer to Ms. Fitt's question!

A PLAGUE OF PESKY PENGUINS

Suddenly the door flew open and the Tardy Boys and the desks tumbled backward. Kids screamed and Leyton curled into a ball on the floor and covered his head with his arms in case penguins were like crows and went for the eyeballs first.

Just then, he heard a loud squeaking sound followed by heavy footsteps and the hissing sweep of a broom.

"Get back, you plague of pesky penguins!" someone shouted.

The voice sounded familiar. Leyton opened his eyes and saw that it was gold-medal custodian Olga Shotput and her giant thirty-six-inch Thunderwear®™ Power Push Sweet Sweep Fine Bristle Push Broom! She was using the broom to sweep back the penguin onslaught!

But how did she get into the room when the penguins were blocking the door?

"Go out the emergency window, children!" Olga shouted as she bravely swept back wave after wave of penguin attackers.

That was it! Leyton realized. She'd come through the emergency window! That's what had made the squeaking sound!

"Hurry!" Olga yelled.

Ms. Fitt stood beside the emergency

window and helped the students out onto the soft green grass in the warm February sun. Standing outside they watched through the windows as gold-medal–winning custodian Olga Shotput continued to sweep the penguins back. Only now that Leyton was gone, the penguins no longer seemed to know what to do. They stood around like businessmen in little blue suits, twisting their heads this way and that. Olga gently swept them out of the room, down the hall, and back to the ice rink.

Outside Ms. Fitt took a deep breath of the warm air and watched an orange-and-brown butterfly flutter by. "It's so nice out here," she said. "Maybe we should continue our class outside."

"But the video says that it's dangerous

outside," said Barton. "We'd be much safer to be inside watching television."

"You're right, Barton," said Ms. Fitt. She went over to the emergency window and held it open. "Okay, students, now that Olga has swept out the penguins, lets go back into the classroom so that we can finish watching today's video."

The students started to climb back into the classroom through the emergency window. When it was Wade's turn, he paused and looked at his reflection in the glass. His hair stretched away from his head like the tendrils of a box jellyfish. *It wouldn't be this way*, he thought, *if I had some penguin oil.*

Back in the classroom, Leyton looked around and realized that someone was missing. "Where's Al-Ian?" he asked.

Daisy quickly pressed her finger to her lips and pointed at the emergency window. Outside, Al-Ian looked like he was going to climb in, but then stopped. Leyton realized he was listening while Fibby, who was also outside, spoke into her cell phone.

THE DEATH VALLEY REFUGE FOR DISPLACED PENGUINS

It wasn't until after school in the Tardy Boys' kitchen that Al-Ian could tell the others what he'd overheard Fibby saying.

"At seven o'clock tonight," Al-Ian said, "a truck from the Thunderwear®™ Penguin Oil Company is going to take away all the penguins."

"I don't think so," said Daisy. "The

Heavily Armed Penguin Protection Commandos wouldn't let that happen."

"That's just it," Al-Ian said. "Fibby's convinced HAPPCO to help her round up the penguins. She told them she's going to transport them all to the Death Valley Refuge for Displaced Penguins. But she's really going to take them all to her father's penguin oil factory."

"We have to stop her," said Daisy.

"But how?" asked Al-Ian. "You saw how heavily armed the HAPPCO people are. If we try to interfere, we're liable to get hurt."

Out of the corner of his eye, Leyton thought he saw his hockey bag move. But that wasn't possible. Hockey bags didn't move on their own.

"There has to be a way," said Daisy.

"Wait a minute," said Wade. "If

Fibby pulls up in a truck that says Thunderwear®™ Penguin Oil Company, won't the HAPPCO people suspect something's wrong?"

"You're right!" Daisy gasped. "And that can only mean one thing!"

"She's coming in a submarine?" Leyton guessed.

"No," said Daisy.

"A spaceship?" guessed Al-Ian.

"No," said Daisy.

"She's digging a tunnel?" guessed Leyton.

"No," said Daisy. "Fibby's going to disguise the truck!"

Leyton and Al-Ian shared a puzzled look. But Wade did not care. He was in despair. Now that Leyton's brain cells were actually there. And this was

completely unfair. Because Wade still had
unruly hair that didn't respond to any
hair care repair.

"What could you disguise a truck as?"
Leyton wondered aloud.

"Maybe a square whale on wheels!"
Al-Ian said.

"No, no, it'll still be a truck,"
Daisy explained. "It just won't say
Thunderwear®™ Penguin Oil Company
on the side. It'll say something else."

"Like 'This Truck Does Not Belong to the
Thunderwear®™ Penguin Oil Company'?"
Leyton guessed.

"Not that," said Daisy.

"How about 'If You Think This Truck
Belongs to the Thunderwear®™ Penguin
Oil Company, You're Wrong'?" said Al-Ian.

"Not that, either," said Daisy.

Once again, out of the corner of his eye,

Leyton saw his hockey bag move. This time he was sure of it. He got up and went over to the bag.

"Where are you going?" asked Wade.

"I'm not going anywhere," said Leyton. "I just want to look in my hockey bag."

"Why?" asked Al-Ian.

"Because something inside it moved," Leyton said.

"What could move in your hockey bag?" asked Daisy.

"Robopuck!" Al-Ian gasped.

"There's no such thing as Robopuck," said Daisy.

"Then maybe a giant alien hockey-stick insect!" said Al-Ian.

The others ignored him. By now they were all staring at Leyton's hockey bag. So when something inside it moved again, they all saw it.

"Oh, my gosh!" said Daisy. "There really *is* something in his bag!"

Everyone crowded around Leyton's hockey bag. Now they could hear a scratching sound coming from inside.

"What's going on?" asked TJ, who'd just gotten home from the elementary school. "Why are you crowded around Leyton's hockey bag?"

"There's something inside it," said Daisy.

"You mean, like hockey gear?" TJ said.

"No, something else," said Leyton. "Something that's moving around and making scratching sounds."

"Someone should open it and see," said TJ.

"You do it," Leyton said.

"No way," said TJ. "You."

Leyton shook his head. "No way."

"Why not?" asked Daisy.

"Because what if Al-Ian's right and it is Robopuck or a giant alien hockey-stick insect?" Leyton asked.

Daisy sighed loudly and unzipped the bag. Suddenly, a little blue penguin popped its head out and started flapping and squawking!

"Oh, my gosh!" Daisy gasped. "There's an angry penguin in your hockey bag!"

LEG ATTACK

Everyone jumped back. The little
penguin wiggled and squirmed out of the
hockey bag. Squawking loudly and
flapping its flippers, it started to waddle
toward Leyton.

"Look out!" Al-Ian cried. "It's going to
attack!"

Everyone backed away in fear. But then
Leyton stopped.

"Careful, Leyton!" Al-Ian cried. "Get back!"

Leyton looked down at the little blue penguin. It didn't even come up to his knee. "What could it possibly do to me?" he asked.

"Peck you in the shin," Al-Ian said.

Leyton looked at the little penguin, and the little penguin looked back at him. It had stopped waddling and squawking. It didn't look like it wanted to peck him. In fact, up close, it didn't look angry at all. It spread its little flippers, waddled closer, and wrapped them around Leyton's calf.

"What's it doing?" TJ asked.

"It's trying to cut off the circulation to Leyton's foot!" Al-Ian cried.

Daisy leaned closer. "No, it's not. It's . . . hugging Leyton's leg."

"Why?" asked Al-Ian.

The little penguin let go of Leyton's leg and backed away. Then it flapped its wings, bowed, spun around, and shook its head.

"Isn't that what Leyton did in the ice rink?" Daisy said.

"But when he did it in the ice rink, it made all the penguins angry," said Al-Ian.

"Maybe not," said Daisy. She flapped her elbows, bowed, spun around, and shook her head. The little penguin cocked its head slightly as if puzzled. Then it shook its head and waddled back to Leyton and hugged his leg again.

"It's not angry!" Daisy gasped. "It's in love with Leyton!"

PENGUINESE

Until now, Wade had not spoken. Nor had he moved from the kitchen table where he'd been sulking. It just wasn't fair that he'd been born with unruly hair.

And what was really frustrating was knowing that the cure for his hair problem was practically at his fingertips. If only there was a way to get penguin oil that didn't involve cooking penguins!

But hearing Daisy say that she thought the little blue penguin was in love with his brother made Wade stop sulking. He said, "What are you talking about?"

"I think I'm beginning to understand," said Daisy. "Flapping your elbows, then bowing, then spinning around, then shaking your head must mean 'I love you' in Penguinese."

"What's Penguinese?" TJ asked.

"The language of penguins," said Al-Ian. "But why would it be in love with Leyton?"

"Well, he is awfully good-looking," said Daisy.

Wade flapped his elbows, bowed, spun around, and shook his head. The little penguin watched carefully, then turned to Leyton and hugged his leg yet again.

"Totally dissed!" Al-Ian grinned.

It's this darn Chronic Unruly Hair Syndrome, Wade thought bitterly.

"Are you saying that the reason all those penguins were chasing Leyton at school was because he told them he loved them?" Al-Ian asked.

"Exactly," said Daisy. "They weren't angry. They were thrilled and enchanted! They were beside themselves with emotion!"

"We get the point," Wade grumbled.

"Not the penguin leader, though," Al-Ian said. "I'm certain he looked really mad."

"Wouldn't you be mad if all the females in your colony suddenly declared their love for a handsome blond stranger?" Daisy asked.

I sure would be, Wade thought angrily.

Meanwhile the little blue penguin held onto Leyton's leg. Leyton bent down and gently patted its head. The little blue penguin looked up at Leyton and blinked its eyes and made a cooing sound.

"That's so cute!" said Al-Ian.

Everyone except Wade shared in the little penguin-human lovefest. Interspecies love vibrations filled the kitchen air. After a while, Daisy gazed up at the kitchen clock and gasped, "We have to go back to school!"

"Why?" asked TJ.

"To save the penguins before Fibby takes them all away to be boiled into penguin oil," Daisy said.

Leyton looked down at the little blue penguin still hugging his leg. "But what about this one?"

Daisy stopped. "We'll take it back with us. And Leyton, you better wear a disguise so that the penguin leader doesn't recognize you."

"Why?" asked TJ.

"Because the penguin leader won't want the other penguins to listen if he knows Leyton is with us," Al-Ian realized. "He won't believe that we're trying to save the penguins. He'll think Leyton is just trying to steal all the females."

"What kind of disguise should I wear?" asked Leyton.

"Do you still have that old yellow rain slicker and mask from Halloween?" Daisy asked.

Leyton did, and he went to get them. When he came back he put the little blue penguin in the pocket of the rain slicker.

"Everyone ready?" Daisy asked.

"You guys go ahead," Wade said. "I'll catch up later."

"Is something wrong?" Daisy asked.

"No," Wade replied. "I just have to take

care of some things before I go back to school."

When Daisy, TJ, Leyton and Al-Ian got back to school, the HAPPCO people were still guarding the ice rink.

"How are we going to get in?" asked Al-Ian.

"That way." Daisy pointed at the entrance to the school, which was open because of the tryouts for *American Super Mega Idol Star Search,* which would be held in the auditorium that night.

Leyton, Al-Ian, and TJ followed her into the school. The halls were brightly lit, but empty. They headed for the rear door to the ice rink.

Suddenly, someone behind them shouted, "Ah-ha! Late again!"

THE MOTHER OF ALL WHACK JOBS

Leyton and the others spun around. Assistant Principal Snout was coming toward them, wearing earplugs, a breathing mask, and latex gloves. He pointed at his wristwatch. "It's six-thirty at night. This is the latest you've ever been! What's your excuse this time?"

"We've already been to school today," said Al-Ian.

Assistant Principal Snout frowned. Then his eyes widened as if he'd realized something. "Excellent! You've finally learned your lesson! You've gotten here early for tomorrow."

Daisy nodded. "*Really* early."

Assistant Principal Snout looked at TJ. "But what are you doing here? You're still going to elementary school."

"I'm practicing being early for when I do come to this school," TJ answered.

"Very good," Assistant Principal Snout said approvingly, and turned away.

"The mother of all whack jobs," Daisy whispered and led the others down the hall to the skating rink. Inside they stopped beside the ice rink wall. On the other side, the penguins stared curiously at them. They didn't recognize Leyton because he was wearing the yellow rain slicker and Halloween mask.

"Who's going to do the talking?" Leyton asked.

"You mean flapping," said Al-Ian.

"I'll try it," Daisy said, and went through the gate and out onto the ice. The male leader of the little blue penguins — the one with the spot on his chest — waddled forward to meet her. Daisy bowed, flapped her elbows, and turned her head from one side to the other.

The leader of the penguins bent over and pecked the ice with his beak. Then he stamped his webbed foot and flapped one flipper and then the other.

"What'd he say?" Al-Ian whispered.

"I think he said that the male penguins are very angry at the handsome blond

human for trying to steal all their females," Daisy said.

"But that's not true!" Leyton gasped from behind the mask.

Daisy pressed a finger to her lips. "Shush. You don't want them to figure out that it's you." She turned to the leader and flapped one elbow, then the other, then nodded, then slid her feet around in a circle. The penguin leader squawked, stamped his foot, then turned his head around in a circle. Both Daisy and the penguin leader communicated that way for a while.

"What's going on?" Al-Ian finally asked.

"I asked him what we could do to make him happy, and he said we would have to hand over Leyton for a sacrifice," Daisy said.

"What!?" Leyton gasped.

Daisy pressed her finger to her lips. "Chill. I told him I didn't think we could do that and he said then at least they should get to peck your eyes out."

Leyton swallowed nervously. "You didn't agree to that, did you?"

"Of course not, silly," said Daisy. "I told him no way. So then he asked if we could help him win the *American Super Mega Idol Star Search*."

"Huh!?" Leyton blurted, caught by surprise.

"That's what they want," Daisy explained.

"Are you kidding?" Al-Ian said. "Don't they want us to fight global warming so that they can get their ice back?"

"Not these penguins," said Daisy. "Little blue penguins live in Australia and New Zealand. They hate ice. But what they hate even more than ice are the emperor and Adélie penguins of Antarctica because those species got to be in movies like *March of the Penguins* and *Happy Feet*. And then, to add insult to injury, the rockhopper penguins got to star in *Surf's Up*. The little blue penguins are really upset that they never get to be in movies. The reason they're here is because they want to try out for *American Super Mega Idol Star Search* tonight."

"That's the craziest thing I ever heard," said Al-Ian.

"Yeah," said TJ. "I thought we were going to *save* the penguins, not help them become stars."

"I disagree," said Daisy. "I think the little blue penguins are right. Why should the emperor, Adélie, and rockhopper penguins get all the glory? That's totally unfair. Try to see it from a little blue penguin's point of view."

Leyton laid down on the concrete floor beside the ice rink.

"What are you doing?" TJ asked.

"Trying to see it from a little blue penguin's point of view," said Leyton. "They only grow about sixteen inches tall, so to see it from their point of view you have to get down here."

Daisy, Al-Ian, and TJ shared uncertain glances.

"Uh, that's not what I meant, Leyton," Daisy said.

Bang! Suddenly the front door to the ice rink flew open and a dozen heavily armed HAPPCO troopers wearing green uniforms stormed in. They were followed by a group of people wearing black Thunderwear®™ Penguin Oil Company jumpsuits and carrying thirty-six-inch Thunderwear®™ Power Push Sweet Sweep Fine Bristle Push Brooms. They wore stockings on their heads to protect their identities. They were followed by Fibby on ice skates.

"What are you doing here?" Fibby demanded when she saw Daisy, Leyton, Al-Ian, and TJ.

"We're here to save the penguins," said Al-Ian.

"No way," Fibby said, skating toward them. "I'm here to save the penguins."

"You're not going to save them," said Daisy. "You're going to take them to your father's company and have them cooked for their oil."

Fibby quickly looked back at the HAPPCO troopers, who were on the other side of the ice rink and hadn't heard what Daisy said. She turned to Daisy and lowered her voice. "So what? They're just a bunch of dumb birds."

In the meantime, the people in the black Thunderwear®™ Penguin Oil Company jumpsuits had begun to use their thirty-six-inch Thunderwear®™ Power Push Sweet Sweep Fine Bristle Push brooms to sweep the penguins toward the front door of the ice rink.

"Wait a minute," said Al-Ian. "What are you doing here anyway? It's only six-thirty and our spy said you weren't supposed to be here until seven o'clock."

"Well, *our* spy told us about *your* plan so we got here early," said Fibby.

"You have a spy, too?" asked TJ.

"Did you think you were the only ones allowed to have them?" Fibby asked.

"But who could your spy be?" Al-Ian asked.

"Oh, my gosh!" Daisy suddenly realized who it had to be.

FIBBY'S SPY

Daisy looked at the people wearing the black Thunderwear®™ Penguin Oil Company jumpsuits and stockings covering their faces. Only one had a stocking that stuck out from his head at strange angles. Daisy pushed open the gate and hurried across the ice. When she got to that person she pulled off the stocking.

"Wade!" she cried.

Leyton and Al-Ian joined Daisy on the ice.

"You're Fibby's spy!?" Al-Ian said in disbelief.

Wade hung his head in shame.

"Why would you spy for Fibby?" asked Leyton.

"Because penguin oil is the only known cure for Chronic Unruly Hair Syndrome," Wade said. "And Fibby said I could have a free lifetime supply if I helped her."

"But then all these sweet, innocent penguins will have to be cooked," said Daisy.

Wade nodded sadly. "I know, Daisy. But I don't think you understand what it's like to go through life with Chronic Unruly Hair."

"It can't be worse than going through life thinking that your skull is so empty that there's room for monkeys to swing from branch to branch," said Leyton.

"Or worse than going through life knowing that at any moment you're going to be kidnapped by aliens," said Al-Ian.

"Or going through life wearing these stupid purple granny glasses because some kid's book author thinks they're cute," said Daisy.

A tear rolled down Wade's cheek. "I'm sorry, guys, but I just couldn't take it anymore. I mean, every morning, looking in the mirror and seeing the same ugly unruly hair. It's hard enough having a good-looking muscular blond twin brother whose flowing blond locks are perfect, but when that cute little penguin rejected me, that was the straw that broke the camel's back."

Leyton started to look around.

"Don't tell me you're looking for a camel," Wade grumbled. Meanwhile, the people wearing the black jumpsuits swept the little blue penguins past them. The penguins were flapping and squawking and fighting, but the brooms were too big and wide.

Suddenly, the little blue penguin in the pocket of Leyton's yellow slicker fought its way out and hopped to the ice in front of Daisy, Leyton, Al-Ian, and TJ. The little penguin stomped its feet and flapped its flippers.

"What's it saying?" asked Al-Ian.

"It's asking why we're letting these bad people sweep all its friends away," Daisy said as she answered the little penguin by stamping her feet and flapping her elbows. "I'm explaining it's because Wade felt bad that it rejected him for Leyton."

The little penguin stomped its feet and flapped its flippers.

"Now what's it saying?" asked Leyton.

"It says that it thinks Wade is cute, but what's with the unruly hair?" Daisy said as she stamped-flapped an answer. "And I'm answering that it's not Wade's fault. It's just that he was born with Chronic Unruly Hair Syndrome."

The little penguin stomped its feet and flapped its flippers.

"Now what's it saying?" asked Al-Ian.

"It asked why Wade doesn't just shave all his hair off?" said Daisy.

"Does it really think men with shaved heads are attractive?" asked Wade.

Daisy quickly acted out the question, and the little blue penguin acted out the answer.

"It says, yes!" Daisy said. "If you shaved

your head, it thinks you'd be just as good-looking as your brother."

"I'll do it!" Wade cried. "And then I won't need penguin oil and I won't have to help send all these cute little penguins to Fibby's father to be cooked."

The little penguin pecked the ice and turned in a circle and did a backward somersault.

"Is it saying it'll like me more than Leyton if I shave my head?" Wade asked hopefully.

"No," said Daisy. "It said hair, schmair, the people from Thunderwear®™ Penguin Oil have swept its whole colony out of the ice rink and if we don't do something fast there's going to be a lot of cooked penguin tonight."

"Come on!" Leyton cried. "We have to stop them!"

JUST FOLLOWING ORDERS

Daisy and the Tardy Boys and Al-Ian ran outside where the people in the black jumpsuits were herding the penguins into the truck. Only the truck was no longer black with THUNDERWEAR®™ PENGUIN OIL COMPANY printed on the side. Now it was bright green with SAVE THE PENGUINS! printed on the side. The heavily armed commandos from HAPPCO were guarding the truck.

Daisy ran up to Sergeant N. Dangered. "Don't let them take the penguins! You have to stop them!"

"Why?" asked Sergeant N. Dangered.

"Because they're not taking the penguins to Death Valley Refuge for Displaced Penguins from the Southern Hemisphere," said Wade. "They're taking them to the Thunderwear®™ Penguin Oil Company to turn them into penguin oil."

"That's ridiculous," said Sergeant N. Dangered. "There's no such thing as penguin oil."

"There is!" Daisy insisted.

"Oh, yeah?" Sergeant N. Dangered chuckled. "What's it used for?"

"It's the world's only known cure for Chronic Unruly Hair Syndrome," said Wade.

Sergeant N. Dangered studied him. "Your hair does look pretty strange. But if penguin oil's the only cure for that mess on your head, then why aren't *you* using it?"

"Because it's wrong to kill animals just so humans can have beautiful, flowing, manageable locks," said Wade.

"True that," said Sergeant N. Dangered. Behind her the bright green Save the Penguins! truck started. A puff of gray exhaust burst from the tailpipe and the engine grumbled.

"You've got to stop them!" said Leyton.

But Sergeant N. Dangered shook her head. "Sorry. My orders are to make sure this truck leaves here safely."

The bright green truck filled with little blue penguins pulled away from the curb. Wade sat down on the sidewalk and held his head in his hands. "I can't believe what I've done!" he moaned. "I've sent all those cute little blue penguins to certain doom just because my hair was unruly! How could I be so stupid and selfish?"

He looked up at the others and asked in an anguished voice: "Will you guys ever forgive me?"

"Not really," said Leyton.

"Yeah, let's face it, Wade, that was seriously selfish," said Al-Ian.

"All those little penguins are gonna die," said TJ. "And it's all your fault."

"I'd feel pretty awful if I were you," said Daisy.

THE NOT-SO-GREAT AUK

The truck filled with penguins continued toward the school exit. Soon it would go through the gates, turn the corner, and disappear forever. The cute little blue penguins would be turned into penguin oil and used by Chronic Unruly Hair Syndrome sufferers the world over to turn their yucky, unruly hair into beautiful, flowing, manageable locks.

And then someday in the future —
when New York and Miami were
underwater thanks to the melting of the
ice caps, and Point Barrow, Alaska, was a
tropical resort destination with palm
trees and sandy beaches — there would
be no more penguins on Earth. They
would have all joined their extinct
brothers and sisters — the dodo, the
passenger pigeon, the great auk, and
the not-so-great auk — in the big rookery
in the sky.

All because of Wade Tardy.

Wade, if you're reading this, you should
feel terrible. I mean, really awful. What
you did was horrible. I don't know
how you can live with yourself. If I were
you, I'd probably run away and never
show my face around here again.

"I'm going to run away and never show my face around here again," Wade Tardy groaned in despair.

Just then a truck horn blared.

Wade looked up. The bright green truck filled with adorable little blue penguins had stopped just inside the school gates. It couldn't go out... because a line of long black limousines was coming in.

"It's *American Super Mega Idol Star Search!*" Al-Ian cried.

THE MOST POISONOUS CREATURE EVER

The people in the black Thunderwear®™ Penguin Oil Company jumpsuits got out of the truck and started to run toward the school. Fibby jumped out of the truck and ran after them.

"What are you doing?" she screamed.

"Trying out for *American Super Mega Idol Star Search*," one of them, a man with red hair, answered.

"But you're supposed to take these penguins to my father's factory," Fibby yelled. "That's your job!"

"Forget it," said the man with red hair. "If I win *American Super Mega Idol Star Search*, I won't need this job anymore."

Meanwhile, the long black limousines stopped in front of The School With No Name, and the famous celebrity judges got out.

"Oh, wow, it's really them!" Fibby gushed and started toward the school herself, instantly forgetting about the penguins.

Daisy turned to the Tardy Boys and Al-Ian. "This is our chance!"

"To try out for *American Super Mega Idol Star Search*?" Leyton asked.

"No, to save the penguins!" Daisy said and ran toward the truck.

The Tardy Boys and Al-Ian followed Daisy to the truck and helped her open the big back doors. Inside, the crowd of penguins stared at her. Daisy flapped her elbows, did three jumping jacks, spun in a circle, and patted the top of her head.

The male penguin leader with the spot on his chest flapped and pecked and crouched.

Daisy stamped her foot, made a fist, and pinched her nose.

The penguin leader shook his head, did a back flip, and curtsied.

"What's going on?" Al-Ian asked.

"I told the leader of the penguins that this was their chance to escape," Daisy said. "And he said that was good because they'd held a meeting in the back of the truck and decided that they wanted to go back to Australia anyway."

"I thought they wanted to try out for *American Super Mega Idol Star Search*," said TJ.

"He said that after getting brushed around by a gold-medal–winning janitor with a special thirty-six-inch Thunderwear®™ Power Push Sweet Sweep Fine Bristle Push Broom and being kidnapped by people from the Thunderwear®™ Penguin Oil Company, they've decided that humans are too dangerous," Daisy said. "They'd rather live on a beach in Australia, even with box jellyfish, than try to survive around humans."

"But box jellyfish are the most poisonous creatures on Earth," said Al-Ian.

"That depends on how you look at it," said Daisy. "We humans think

box jellyfish are the most poisonous
creatures on Earth. But if you ask the
rest of the animal kingdom, know what
they'd say?"

"That humans are the most poisonous
creatures?" Wade realized.

"True that," said Daisy. "We've
destroyed more natural habitats
and created more poisons and bombs and
pollution than any other creature in
history. Box jellyfish have killed a few
thousand humans, but only humans have
wiped out entire species."

"Plus, with all our wars and pollution
we've managed to kill millions of other
humans as well," said TJ.

"At the rate we're going, we'll probably
make ourselves extinct someday," said
Al-Ian.

"True that," said everyone else.

"But how are the little blue penguins going to get back home?" asked TJ.

"I'll ask," Daisy said, and did sign language with the leader of the penguins. "He said they got a ride here on a ship. He said there are always ships going back to Australia. All we have to do is get them to the port and they'll find one."

"But none of us knows how to drive," said Leyton.

"And everyone who does know how to drive is too busy trying out for *American Super Mega Idol Star Search*," said Al-Ian.

"Not everyone!" Wade said, and ran toward the school. A moment later, he returned with gold-medalist janitor Olga Shotput.

"Wade told me that the penguins weren't trying to attack you in the classroom," she said. "They only wanted to get to Leyton because they loved him. Now I feel terrible for brushing them back with my thirty-six-inch Thunderwear®™ Power Push Sweet Sweep Fine Bristle Push Broom. How can I show them how sorry I am?"

"Can you drive them to the port and make sure they get on a ship back to Australia?" asked Daisy.

Gold-medalist janitor Shotput clicked her heels and saluted. "It would be an honor!"

A few moments later Olga drove away in the bright green Save the Penguins! truck, loaded with little blue penguins on their way home. By now, almost everyone had crowded into The School With No Name to try to become America's next Super Mega Idol Star. Even the HAPPCO commandoes and Lucy Lipps were trying out.

But the Tardy Boys and their friends started to walk toward their homes because they didn't need to be stars to be happy. In the trees, birds who had not bothered to go south for the winter sang their evening songs. Moths fluttered to and fro in the warm February dusk air.

"Know what's funny?" Daisy asked.

"A fat lady with a skinny husband?" TJ guessed.

"No," said Daisy.

"All the unruly hair left on the floor after you shave your head?" guessed Wade.

"No."

"The answer to the question, Why don't penguins fly?" guessed Al-Ian.

"No."

"Wait," said TJ. "What is the answer?"

"They can't afford plane tickets," said Al-Ian.

"But that's not what's funny," said Daisy.

"Well, it is kind of funny," said Wade.

"But that's not what I was talking about when I asked what was funny," said Daisy.

"Then what were you talking about?" asked Leyton.

"What's funny is that Fibby had the truck painted with SAVE THE PENGUINS! when she really didn't want to save them," said Daisy. "But in the end, the truck saved the penguins after all."

"That's actually kind of ironic," said Wade.

"But funny, too," said Al-Ian.

"More ironic than funny," said Wade.

"No," said Al-Ian. "More funny than ironic."

"How many people think it's more ironic than funny?" asked Wade.

Leyton and TJ raised their hands.

"How many people think it's more funny than ironic?" asked Al-Ian.

Daisy and Leyton raised their hands.

"You can't raise your hand for both," said Wade.

"Why not?" asked Leyton.

"Because it's one or the other."

"But I have two hands," said Leyton.

"It doesn't matter," said Wade.

"It doesn't matter that I have two hands?" asked Leyton.

"No, it wouldn't matter if you have *three* hands," said Wade. "You can only raise your hand once."

"But I've raised my hand lots of times," said Leyton.

"That's not the point," said Wade.

"What is the point?" asked Leyton.

"The point is the really sharp part," said Al-Ian.

"Sometimes it's the part that sticks out into the water," said Daisy.

"Sometimes it's what dogs do," said TJ.

"Dogs point?" said Al-Ian.

"With their noses," said TJ.

"I'd like to point out that this has nothing to do with the point I was making," said Wade.

"Good point," said Daisy.

And thus the Tardy Boys and their friends walked into the warm February sunset having a lively debate about a point that none of them could recall. And so the fourth book in their series comes to an end.

True that.

ACKNOWLEDGMENTS

If you have read the previous books in the Tardy Boys series, then you know that the author likes to acknowledge rich and famous people like Tenzing Norgay, Carlos Slim Helu, and the inventor of Silly Putty, who was either Dr. Earl Warrick, Peter Hodgson, or James Wright, depending on which Internet site you believe.

The author doesn't actually know any rich and famous people, but he hopes that if he keeps acknowledging them, one of them will take pity on him and become his friend.

Let's face it, there are a lot of advantages to being friends with someone who is rich and famous. You might get to ride in his or her limousine, or fly in his or her private jet. And you can be pretty sure that whenever you go to his or her house there'll be plenty of good stuff to eat in the refrigerator (unless your rich and famous friend is a movie star or fashion model, in which case there'll be nothing but celery, fat-free yogurt, and bottled water).

In the past books in this series, the author has acknowledged both Catherine Zeta-Jones and Scarlett Johanssen in the hope that they would take pity on him and become his friends. But neither has (yet). Do you know someone rich and famous? Do you think he or she would like to be the author's friend? If so, please have them write to:

The Author
P.O. Box XOXO
Fingers Crossed, New Mexico

IS That a Dead Dog in Your Locker?

When Leyton and Wade Tardy agree to help their friend Daisy hide a dog at school, they have no idea what they're getting themselves into. Wheezy is just a small dog, but he leaves a BIG stink behind wherever he goes! With the NFA (No Furry Animals) rule at their school, hiding Wheezy is going to be very tricky and very smelly. Fibby Mandible, the school's bossiest, snobbiest girl, is hot on the Tardy Boys' trail, and so is Barton Slugg, the WORST ARCHENEMY EVER! Can Wade and Leyton keep Wheezy a secret, or will his awful stench give him away?

Is That a Sick Cat in Your Backpack?

There's something strange about Leyton and Wade Tardy's pet cat. Skinny Cat is the scrawniest, scraggliest, laziest cat ever, but he has one very big, very disgusting talent—he can cough up hair balls like a champ! But will that be enough for him to win the school's Catalent Contest? Not if Fibby Mandible, the school's bossiest, snobbiest girl, and Barton Slugg, the WORST ARCHENEMY EVER, have anything to say about it! But the Tardy Boys never give up, and when the Catalent Contest turns into a battle to save the entire world, it's up to them to come to the rescue.

Is That a Glow-in-the-Dark Bunny in Your Pillowcase?

With Halloween approaching, Leyton and Wade Tardy are trying to come up with totally awesome costumes. Whoever has the best costume will win The School With No Name's King of Candy Contest. Unfortunately, Fibby Mandible, the school's bossiest, snobbiest girl, and Barton Slugg, the WORST ARCHENEMY EVER, have their eyes on that prize as well. And when the fiercest, meanest, most sinister aliens in the entire universe appear in their neighborhood, only Wade and Leyton can save the Earth from being destroyed.

Also by Todd Strasser

*Mysterious video games, ghost trains,
and phantom text messages . . .
Better leave the lights on!*